I0686914

Yellow Bird

Linda Johnson

A Garden Gate Farm publication

Published by Garden Gate Farm 2010

Copyright © 2010 by Garden Gate Farm

All rights reserved. No part of this book may be used or reproduced in any manner whatsoever without written permission from the publisher, except in the case of brief quotations embodied in critical articles and reviews.

First Edition, June 2010
First Edition, Second Printing, October 2010
Second Edition, August 2011

Library of Congress Control Number: 2010915885

ISBN 978-0-578-06973-9

A work of the imagination, written and designed by Linda Johnson

"Johnson's debut is, at its core, a pastoral tale, a celebration of the rustic music and rich traditions of the hills and hollows of Virginia and West Virginia and their ability to offer relief and purpose in a harsh, lonesome world. . . a charming story about a bygone time where even magic seems possible."

— *KIRKUS REVIEWS*

DEDICATED TO

Dave, Liza, Josie, Mia, Jack,
and all who come before and after.

The night was dark by this time as it would be until morning; what light we had, seemed to come more from the river than the sky, as the oars in their dipping struck at a few reflected stars.

~ Charles Dickens, *Great Expectations*

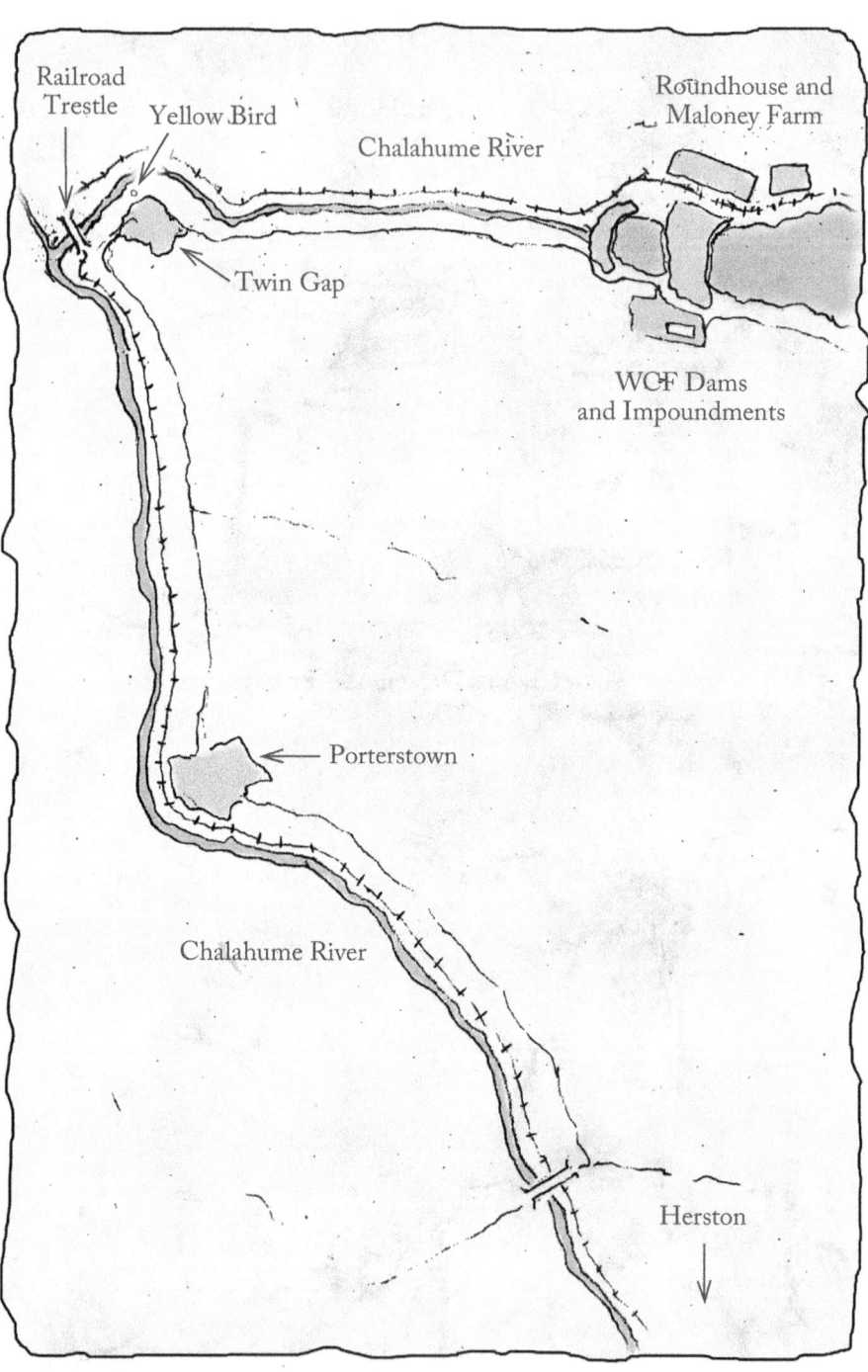

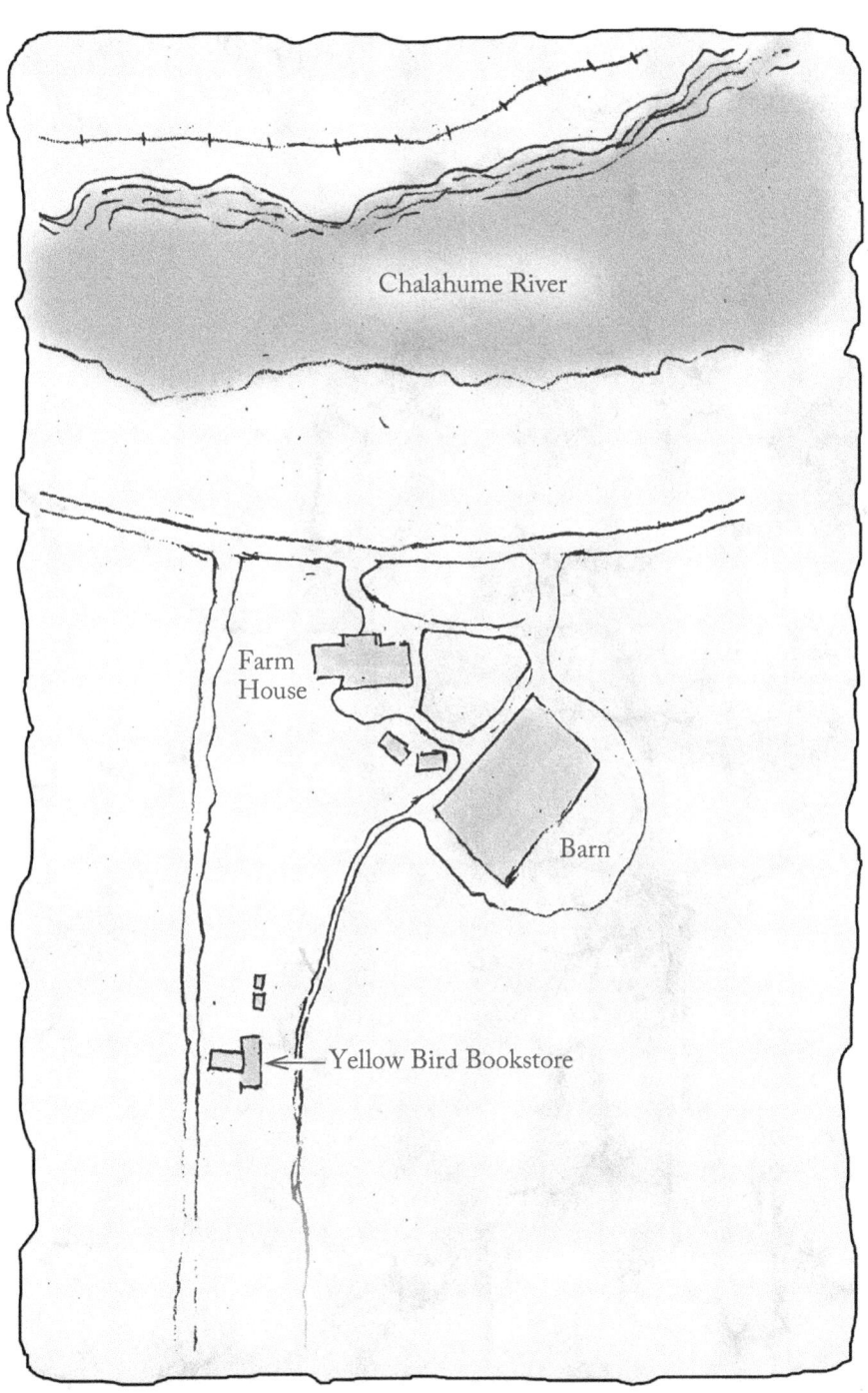

Chalahume River

Farm
House

Barn

Yellow Bird Bookstore

Book One

She gazed the heavens blue and bare
longing to belong up there
when on her thoughts a restless nest
drew points of stardust on her breast
and she wondered
could she house
the heavens hosted on her blouse
unyielding glory diadem
pulsing life then dies again
in and out the breath of tides
within her lungs sing mystified
resounding call
the net is cast
a knotted tongue unfurled at last

Beyond the shore the sea runs through
an old man's well-worn solitude
he tamps his pipe then packs it new
he lights a match
a spark it flew
with all his toil hammered out
upon the years he cast without
a glance behind a forward look
and now a thought of life forsook

She thought it odd when she awoke
feeling that the heavens spoke
and when she paused to ponder this
a shooting star flew from her breast

1

It had been a tough year for the Yellow Bird, Amanda's used
bookstore, a clapboard building painted ochre years ago over a coat of
whitewash that showed through. It was a small building with a long
history, rumored to be named for a native woman who had saved a
settler's child from drowning in the Chalahume River that tumbled
through the gorge behind the farm at Twin Gap.

In the beginning, the Yellow Bird was a cider inn, quenching
thirsty travelers passing through on the wagon trail to the Scots-Irish
and English settlements further up on South Mountain. When the
railroad came through a century later, Twin Gap became a popular
destination, especially for the well heeled who sought to escape the
heat of the city or yearned for the unsurpassed beauty of the Appala-
chians. In more recent years, the romance of the passenger train had
given way to the hard practicality of coal, and the Yellow Bird now
depended on the generosity of sightseers who ventured off Interstate 81 to take their chances on the back roads along the Virginia
and West Virginia border on their way to the more popular summer
resorts in Tennessee.

Amanda sat out back on the bookstore's large stone patio laid
more than a hundred years ago with blue and gray granite from the
old abandoned quarry at the edge of the coal mine. She rested her

elbows on a massive hand-hewn table and held a worn and stained brochure from the 1920s. She opened it to a picture of a string of guests lined shoulder-to-shoulder at this very table. They were wearing the white gabardine and seersucker of the day, parasols and bonnets aflutter. Amanda's grandmother was standing behind them ladling out bowls of soup while the patrons smiled white-toothed into the camera. The caption read: "The Yellow Bird is an unlikely retreat for the well-to-do nature enthusiast." She was certain her grandmother had charged handsomely for their soiree in the mountains.

Her grandmother looked as stalwart and weathered as an old boot, but she couldn't have been older than thirty. Life had been hard for Bernie, which is what everybody called her grandmother. By then she already had been widowed for five years, maybe more, and was left with a baby, Amanda's mother, to raise alone.

Amanda pulled out the only other photograph she had of her grandmother. It was from an earlier time, taken at the beach when she was just a teenager. Even through the fading and mottled image, Amanda could see that Bernie was a strikingly beautiful woman, teasing the camera with a devil-may-care pose, all legs and curves. Amanda looked at the pictures side by side and sighed, wondering if she was destined to suffer the same fate. She knew as well as anybody how a few short years could change a person.

How had her grandmother managed it – the farm, the bookstore, a daughter? Amanda was barely hanging on, even without a child in tow. And the truth was, it was getting harder. Too hard. Soon even Bernie, from the other side of the grave, would have to admit that.

Amanda turned to stoke the small fire she'd lit in the patio's stone hearth. The coals came alive against the chill of a dimming sky. She leaned back and sipped a home brew, letting her thoughts wander as they would, a healing hand over the memory of the past few months.

"Pardon me, ma'am," he said, standing on her patio in the half shadow and angled light of the doorway, and she swung around to see who it was. "The door was open so I let myself in," he said, hat in hand. "I'm just passin' through and need somethin' to read."

She thought she recognized him and started to get up, but she sat down again and looked at him more carefully. No, she was mistaken, she didn't know him after all. "Sorry, we're closed" is the only thing she could think of to say. What kind of man suddenly materializes on a stranger's doorstep? Especially on Sunday. And besides, she was closed for the season. Everyone knew it. What was he really after?

"I'm only here for a book, if you don't mind the inconvenience," he continued.

"We're closed," she said again. He wasn't very tall. Maybe five feet ten. She figured she could take him down if she had to. Working the farm had one advantage. It kept her small frame strong and agile. Yet he didn't seem dangerous. On the contrary, he was open and congenial and appeared genuine. Her hesitation seemed to amuse him, and that rattled her. She looked away realizing she'd been staring at him for a long time. Again he smiled, this time broadly. One thing she could tell for sure, this was a man accustomed to the silent and thorough scrutiny of a woman.

"Yeah, you told me." He ran his fingers through his curly brown hair and it made her pause. Something about that small gesture felt familiar. He felt familiar. But then again, he didn't.

"You been here before?" she asked.

He shrugged. He wore a patch over his right eye. Injuries were common up and down the ridge, especially these days. Between the coal mines, farms, and railroad, there was hardly a soul who didn't live with some sort of disfigurement. She was about to ask him what had happened, when he said, "I'd like to pay for a couple of books I picked out in there. And maybe a couple of those." He pointed to her beer. "You sell in bottles?"

He passed the litmus test, for now anyway. She nodded and got up from the table.

"So what'd you pick out?" she asked, showing him back into the shop.

"Does it matter?"

"Maybe, maybe not. I find it interesting, though – what people choose."

He slid the books across the counter. "How do I measure up?"

She rang up a T.S. Elliot collection: not bad, she thought. Then a 1959 copy of *Houdini: The Man Who Walked Through Walls* and a 1937 edition of *Margery Wilson's Pocket Book of Etiquette: The Modern Social Guide*.

"I have eclectic tastes," he said and he pulled out a pack of Camels.

"Don't light up in here," she said.

He nodded then tucked the pack into his shirt pocket.

I know this man, she thought. "That'll be seven dollars and thirty-nine cents."

"Tax included?"

"Everything included, but you get a five cent refund if you return those bottles."

"Thank you, ma'am," he said with a tip of his hat. "I just might do that." And he disappeared out the door.

2

His name was Jeremiah Abner Stone, but he'd been called Cody for as long as he could remember. It had been nearly a year since he was discharged from the army and six months since he'd been released from the hospital.

The flesh just above his knee had been splayed by shrapnel and had healed well enough. After two operations and some physical therapy he could almost walk without a limp. But the incessant standing is what still killed him. He'd have to get another job soon if the boss couldn't find any sitting-down work for him to do.

It was an honorable discharge and he left the documents with his mother in case he ever needed to prove it. He came stateside feeling a lot of things, but honorable wasn't one of them. He'd only been on tour for three months when it happened. He was one of four in an advance team sent to sweep the village before the rest of the company arrived. Reconnaissance assured them that the town had been abandoned, but sabotage had become a more frequent ploy of the guerrillas and the lieutenant was taking extra precautions. Twice last week, they received news of troops not far north losing men in maneuvers like this. A pattern was emerging. Insurgents invade a town, terrorize the villagers, cleanse the population, then leave behind a maze of landmines to detonate when a door opens or a foot steps carelessly off the designated path.

It was Cody's first serious assignment and he was terrified. He was ashamed of his fear but he couldn't shake it. It seized him like a wild animal the moment they left the jeep and started the long dark hike to the village.

They'd been told the town was strategic. It was the only viable route to the bridge beyond it. His company would cross over, destroy the bridge, and then rendezvous with the rest of the regiment about ten miles south.

Cody's buddy, a colored man named Clarence Robinson, spotted the house first. It emerged from the night when they rounded the bend. It was a simple thatched building along the side of the road with a dilapidated shed in the back. Clarence moved out ahead of the rest and Cody soon followed. His sweat smelled sour and it poured from his armpits and down his back. He felt nauseous. It wasn't supposed to be like this. He had prepared.

Mr. Edgeworth was the one who delivered Cody's draft notice. He wasn't their regular postman, but having served in the last war, Mr. Edgeworth insisted on handing the message to Cody himself. He lingered while Cody and his mother read it.

"When do you report, son?" Mr. Edgeworth asked.

"In four weeks," Cody told him.

"Then start preparin' now," he advised. "You'll be all right if you're prepared." He turned to Mrs. Stone and squeezed her hand. "He'll be all right, ma'am, don't you worry," and he headed back down the road to finish his route.

Cody heeded the warning. He would prepare. A thick skin was the best defense against whatever lay ahead. He began to read accounts of war, war of any kind. The Peloponnesian Wars. Sparta. The Civil War with all its blood and brutality. The Great War and the stories told by victims of chemical poisoning. Reels of Churchill entering the German camps. Hiroshima. The bombing of North Korea. The more gruesome the better so he would be ready to face the Viet Cong. But he was not ready.

When they reached the thatched house, Clarence began to check the side window for wires and trips, then he climbed through. Several long numbing seconds passed before Cody heard Clarence whisper, "It's empty." Cody looked in the window. The blue light of the moon shone through and Cody could just make out Clarence's silhouette in the hallway leading to a room in the rear. Cody slipped out of sight and began circling to the back of the house.

He moved silently over the dirt, every muscle taught, his rifle erect, the butt pressed firmly on his shoulder. He could hear his blood pulsing in his ears. He stopped at the end of the wall and listened. Nothing. He gulped his breath and then held it. Slowly he pushed his face around the corner and aimed his rifle into the night. Nothing.

The back of the house was in shadow. He could see a door with a small opened window beside it. He peered in but it was too dark to see. All was silence. He told himself to be patient. The darkness was disorienting and he thought he might faint. But he did not. He knew Clarence would be taking his time surveying every inch of the hallway for traps. Cody tried to stop shaking while he waited for him. Gradually his pupils, already dilated with fear, opened and a small mound in the corner of the room came into focus.

There on the floor piled in a heap were the bodies; limbs and necks bent at odd angles, faces contorted, eyes blank. Small bodies. Boys and girls. Motionless, inert, dead. Left there for him to find. And he did find them. He started to vomit. At that moment, a single moment plucked from the infinite sea of moments floating unnoticed past the rest of the world, Cody's soul shattered into a million pieces.

"Jesus Christ!" Clarence screamed as he entered the room. Cody's reflexes took over. In one swift leap, he kicked open the door. It was the last thing he remembered until he woke up in triage.

"They still don't know why you weren't blown to bits," Clarence joked from the side of the hospital bed weeks later. But Cody *was* blown to bits, the pieces simply hadn't surfaced yet. He could hear Clarence talking but couldn't figure out how to answer him or anyone else for that matter. It was as if he had become an ice melt, breaking up and slowly drifting farther and farther away in every direction from everyone and everything he had ever known. A million pieces unreachable and unredeemable.

"They say it's shellshock. Not your leg, you're nearly over that. They say it's in your head. How'd you do it, man? They're actually going to send you home."

Home to what, Cody wondered.

3

It felt like flying. The upward lift; gravity giving way to her ascent; up and up; the thrill of weightlessness. Soaring through the cold blue sky, her heart thumping wildly, her limbs buoyant, her body graceful in its trajectory. Eternity hung from this moment, this point, this apex, where everything stops, everything ceases, everything is forever.

It felt like that. She remembered now.

Amanda woke up in the hospital. The room was dim with light leaking through the blinds. It smelled like soap, wax, and pee. She felt her mother's hand on her forehead in the way she used to check for fever when she was little. Her head wasn't hot but it was pounding from the inside out. She groaned. Her mother called for more pain medication. She fell asleep again.

Jesse was in the room. Amanda couldn't open her eyes but she could hear his voice. He was talking to her parents.

"She was banging on my door, mad as a hornet," he told them. "I asked her what was wrong. She just needed to burn off some steam, is what she said. You know how Amanda gets when she's mad."

Way to go, Jess, Amanda thought. It was beginning to sound like a confession.

"Turns out, I was getting ready to meet Lyle up at Kreeger Bluff to do some dirt-biking. She insisted on coming along so we jumped in the truck and took off."

Great, Amanda thought, like I wasn't in enough trouble.

"When we got up there and unloaded the bikes, Amanda said she wanted to ride. I told her to hop on but she said no, she wanted to go by herself. I told her it was a stupid idea because she hadn't driven a bike before and these trails were pretty steep. But she didn't care. 'Gotta learn sometime and there's no time like the present,' she said. I could tell she wasn't going to budge so I showed her what to do."

He found the wheelchair from the corner of the room and grabbed the handles. "I showed her how to give it gas," he said, bearing down with his wrists and thrusting the chair forward. "And how to brake." Amanda's mother jumped aside as he careened to a stop at the far side of the room.

The nurse flew in the doorway. "Young man, if you can't be quiet, I'll have to ask you to leave."

"Yes, ma'am," Kyle said. He sat in the wheelchair, leaned forward, and whispered, "I showed her how to kill the gas if the throttle got stuck, which it did sometimes. She circled the truck a few times to get the feel of it. Then she grabbed my helmet and took off. She sped up the path that ran under the high-tension wires. She was going way too fast, that's for sure. She made it to the top okay but there's a boulder that juts out across the peak and she hit it too hard. That's when the bike went airborne and so did she. She just sailed straight through the air," he said, his arm indicating her flight pattern.

"She was standing when we got up there but she didn't know where she was. She knew me but didn't recognize Lyle. We carried her back down the mountain but by the time we got to the truck she passed out again. We didn't know what to do so we drove her here." He sat down and exhaled. "That's when we called you."

Amanda was released the following day. A bad concussion, they said. Except for the memory loss and headaches, which they claimed were temporary, she would be okay.

4

The cold was fierce. Sharp gusts of icy wind pierced through Amanda's clothes and stung her legs. That was the first thing she noticed. That and the hard white glare of the sun.

The gravel under her feet crackled on the frozen ground. "Why did I wear my favorite suede shoes on a day like this?" she thought. Already bits of ice and dust were collecting on the toes, melting into greasy stains.

Her mother was wearing her black boots with the two-inch heels and they punched through the thin crust of snow leaving a trail of holes behind her. Her father was walking next to her mother, which was curious. They rarely did that anymore.

"You know Bernie wouldn't have wanted me to come," he whispered, his breath freezing to his thick glasses. "Guess I've had the last laugh after all."

Her mother shrugged and kept her gaze upon the path that circled up a small crest, opening to a little tree-line park at the top. Even though the pace was slow, her mother was breathing harder than usual and her nostrils looked like little chimneys pumping out smoke. The cold made her eyes red along the rims and her lashes were frozen together in little points.

Amanda glanced over her shoulder. A dozen or so people were

walking behind them. She didn't recognize them but they smiled at her anyway.

When they reached the top of the hill, she could see a few rows of white plastic chairs aligned on a length of green tarp. In front of them a blue canopy was stretched tautly on metal poles protecting a freshly dug grave.

"Who died?" Amanda whispered to her mother as they found their places in the front row. Her mother hugged her hard, and she could smell the perfume her mother wore on special occasions.

"Remember? It's your grandmother."

"Bernie?" A particularly biting gust cut through the tent and they braced against it as they shuffled into their seats.

"All right if I sit here?" came a muffled voice through a woolen scarf. It was Amanda's friend Dehlia, whom she'd known since she was little.

Her mother nodded. "Please. I wish you would."

"What are you doing here?" Amanda asked when Dehlia sat down.

"What are you talking about? Let's see, I don't know, I heard it was going to be a good show. I didn't have a ticket so I crashed the gate." She blew on her hands. "Your grandmother died, you dope."

Amanda nodded.

Dehlia shook her head. "Wow, you really did knock your brains out, didn't you?"

They sat in their chairs, resigned to the solemn mood that was settling in. "So when did she die?" Amanda asked her.

Across the gravesite the sun had not yet crept above the tent and its low refraction had a darkening effect on Amanda's eyes leaving people and things strangely illuminated upon a background of shadow. In front of them, a robed man stood in silhouette thumbing through a bible, each page backlit and exposed to the cold light. Next to him, rays careened off four silver posts that stood on each corner of the grave. A shimmering black festoon hung around it concealing a contraption that would eventually lower her grandmother into her final resting place.

She looked again at the people around her and it occurred to her that she *did* know them after all. Dehlia's parents, Mr. and Mrs.

Greene, were there, along with her little brother, Sam, looking utterly miserable at having been made to come. Further down the row, she saw some aunts and uncles on her mother's side, the type of relatives that only appear at reunions and weddings. And funerals also, she concluded. And she also noticed a lot of empty chairs.

"It's not the heat," her father said to her mother in low tones. "It's the humidity."

Her mother didn't turn and she didn't speak, but her face betrayed her. She still enjoyed that about him, even though they'd been divorced a long time. The scandalous comments at inopportune times. He'd do it to keep her spirits up, to help steel her against hard times. "It's just like her to pick a day like this," he added as he leaned back in his chair.

Off in the distance on the other side of the gravesite, a shiny new 1968 black hearse appeared on the horizon, its windshield blinking randomly in the sunlight. It lumbered slowly toward them, across the rolling cemetery lawns, weaving through the massive mausoleums that rose formidably from the frozen landscape.

The preacher tucked his Bible under one arm and signaled with the other. The pallbearers—Amanda's father, Mr. Greene, and a few cousins—lined up along the side of the tent. The hearse pulled up to the clearing and the driver leaped out. He grabbed the preacher by the elbow and led him to the back of the hearse. The preacher looked inside and then quickly reappeared over the door, wide-eyed and flushed, carefully surveying the grave. When he spotted Amanda's mother staring at him from the front row, he blinked, took a deep breath, and nodded to the driver, "Thank you, sir, but I will take it from here."

With slow deliberate steps, the preacher approached the pallbearers. As he spoke, Amanda could see her cousins shuffle about nervously, and her father tipped back in his shoes with what looked like anticipation. Then the little group disbanded and took their seats again.

At last, the preacher reached into the hearse and emerged carrying a cardboard shoebox tied with a bright green ribbon. Amanda's mother blanched as he proceeded toward the gravesite holding between his palms the boxed remains of her grandmother.

"She always loved that shade of green," whispered her father.

"Oh shut up, Randy," her mother shouted. "I don't know what's happened. When she started calling around to funeral parlors, I told her *I'd* make the arrangements. I even showed her the casket I picked out, a very nice casket. What kind of a person makes their own funeral arrangements?"

People began to fidget in their chairs and Amanda could hear her aunts exchanging words. Her mother tried to get up but her father pressed his hand on her shoulder and she sat down again.

The preacher continued his ceremonious march toward the other side of the tent where he could get a better look at the grave. A few wide straps spanned the hole, poised to receive Bernie's casket, but they were too slack to hold the little box. In a notable spurt of improvisation, the preacher turned on his heels, held the box skyward, and intoned a prayer from his silent but moving lips. Then ever so solemnly he lowered his charge onto the top of one of the grave's corner posts. And there sat her grandmother. Perched like a green parrot ready to scold whoever was responsible for making these expensive and unnecessary arrangements.

With the sleeve of his robe, the preacher dabbed at the condensation on his brow. He turned to face his audience, "Dearly beloved," he began.

"Guess she got the last laugh after all," her father said.

5

A week after the funeral, Amanda and Dehlia met at the Claw, the café down the street from the campus where her father and Dehlia's mother taught. The caffeine had a beneficial effect on Amanda's headaches, at least it seemed like it, and she was on her third cup just to make sure. Dehlia was working on a cherry bomber which glowed like neon through the straw.

"It's still hard to believe your grandmother's dead," she said between slurps. "I thought she'd be around forever."

"I know. I can't believe it either. She was a weird old lady and so ridiculously irritating."

"That's an understatement," Dehlia said. "She was petulant."

Dehlia was always trying on words, the way other people tried on clothes. "I know." Amanda said. "Seems like she saved her dying breath just to harass me. I wonder how she stayed so focused on giving me a hard time even when she was sick."

"Did you ever remember what she did to make you so mad?"

"Yeah, sort of. We'd been building up to it. During those last few weeks she'd been needling me relentlessly. Every time I entered the room it was 'Amanda, consider you choices, your future. The Yellow Bird is where you belong. Don't ever forget it.'" Amanda leaned toward Dehlia, looked down her nose, and resumed pitching her sentences across the table the way Bernie used to. " 'Your path is an important one, Amanda, stay on it. You're a torch carrier, Amanda. It's about time you acted like one.'

" 'I'm just 17 years old, Bernie' I screamed at her. 'I don't care if you *are* dying' I said. 'That's no excuse for being so mean. Go ahead and die already and leave me alone.'"

Dehlia's cherry bomber drained from her straw and she stared at Amanda.

"I know," Amanda said. "Nice bedside manner, huh? After that I stomped out and slammed the door behind me. It was the last time I saw her. Guess I won't be winning the granddaughter-of-the-year award."

Dehlia shook her head. "That's pretty awful, Amanda, even for you. Your timing was atrocious but I have to say, it sounds like she had it coming. Maybe she went ahead and died right then just to make you feel worse."

"No I don't think so. She and I both knew her time was close though. We talked about it. Remember that week when my mom made that business trip and left me to take care of her? We talked about it then."

Amanda's mother sold medical equipment and she traveled a lot. At least she did before Bernie moved in. When this particular trip to Chicago came up, her mother said she couldn't get out of it, and she informed Amanda that she would be caretaker while her mother was gone.

The week started out fine. Amanda stayed busy getting used to the routine. Weak tea and broth to start off the morning. "It will improve my digestion, or what's left of it," Bernie told her. She was getting thinner. Her skin was turning to parchment and her face seemed to hang free of her skull in places, yet her eyes still sparkled in their receding sockets. Her long bony fingers lifted the cup and her mouth made a little knot when she blew on the soup. "Too hot, Amanda. Make me a fruit drink while I let this cool. I could use the sugar."

Her mother had situated a plastic toilet behind a curtained screen on the other side of the room so Bernie wouldn't have to climb the stairs to go to the bathroom. Now she even had trouble walking that far and Amanda had to help her. "Not much dignity in getting old, Amanda," she said when she caught her glancing at her bum through a gap in her gown.

"No, I guess not," Amanda chuckled.

Most of the day was taken up with similar tasks. Fetching medicine, preparing meals, cleaning sheets, giving sponge baths. Not glamorous stuff but Amanda didn't mind it. As long as she could get outside when she wanted to, she was all right. Which made the errands a welcome relief.

The grocery store was a regular stop. As was the library. Her grandmother was an insatiable reader and she sent Amanda searching for books about almost anything: fairy tales of the ancient Celts. How to grow an avocado. What really happened at Roswell? The theories of Edmund Burke. She wanted to know the origins of the Chinese language and what lived at the bottom of the ocean. Who *was* afraid of Virginia Wolff anyway? And what was all this about black holes? Every day she sent Amanda on another adventure and she came back with arms full of books.

The best day Amanda ever remembered having with Bernie was about mid-week when they got snowed in. Overnight the snow had piled up leaving at least a foot or two on the streets and sidewalks. By afternoon it was still coming down and the thick gray sky showed no signs of relenting. Bernie had eaten a good lunch and was feeling unusually well. "What are you reading?" she asked Amanda.

"It's one of your books about the healing arts in medieval Europe."

"I can see that by the cover. What are you reading *about?*"

"Well, apparently there was an obscure monk who lived in the Balkan Mountains during the 1400s who befriended a Turkish prince. The prince was injured when he fell off his horse in a treacherous mountain notch that passed close to the monk's cloister. The monk found the unconscious prince and lifted him back onto his horse. He secured him to the saddle and then led the horse carefully up the steep slope to the monastery. The prince woke in the monk's bed weeks later fully recovered."

"Well?"

"Well, what?"

"Well what happened? How'd he do it?"

"I don't know, I haven't gotten that far yet."

"You can't leave a story hanging like that. Get up here and read it to me."

"Okay," and Amanda climbed on the bed next to her.

It was dark when Amanda finished the last page. Bernie was asleep. It was a fascinating story, as it turned out. By the prince's account, his injury was so severe he never should have survived at all, and as proof he would display a crater-like depression in the crown of his head to anyone who challenged his story.

The monk was conducting experiments far beyond the science of the day. Up on top of those rural mountains he had built a laboratory in an abandoned chapel that lay on the outskirts of the monastery grounds. High in the bell tower, he had fashioned thick chiseled windows that acted as huge prisms when the sun rose and set over the expansive horizon. Working with the angle of the sun through the window, the monk would cause the room to fill with a particular color of light – from rose to green to violet – depending on the time of day. The monk asserted that every light angle (or spectrum we call it now) lent a healing property to specific ailments: red for blood disease; blue for tumors; yellow for tissue repair; and so on. The prince claimed that the monk had written a compendium of hundreds of remedies that he had proven on the other monks in his order, as well as on the animals they kept.

Twice a day, at the yellow time, the monk had wheeled the prince's cot into the bell tower exposing him to the concentration of rays. Results were slow at the onset, healing deep in the wound first, then progressing more quickly as the inner layers of skin were repaired.

After two weeks, the prince woke with a ravenous appetite and his strength restored. When the prince prepared to depart, he asked the monk how he could return his kindness. The monk would accept no payment for his good deeds and he bid the prince farewell. The prince returned to the mountain notch many times in the course of his travels but he never found the cloister again. The monk and his compendium were forever lost, short of the telling of the prince's story.

Amanda lay on the bed next to her grandmother in the dark

house with the snow banking outside and discovered for the first time how much she loved storytelling. Good stories, old stories, preposterous stories, tall tales, mysterious legends, hidden treasures, unbelievable feats, outrageous calamity, unthinkable domains. If Bernie gave her nothing else, she would always remember that she gave her this.

6

Amanda and her mother sat in the lawyer's office on straight-backed mahogany chairs upholstered in stiff brocade. Mr. Crenshaw, the stout gentleman who sat on the other side of an expansive desk, was like a character from another century. He peered at them over half-moon spectacles and his thin hair glistened under a lacquer of spray that had been applied liberally to his balding head. His well-manicured hands clutched a folder, which, besides a calendar and pen set, was the only thing on his desk.

"You have my deepest sympathy," he began. "These are sad times and I understand how difficult this can be. Still I am glad you could both be here today. She would have wished it so," he said, his face a rehearsed display of woe.

They stared back blankly. Amanda wasn't sure what he expected, but if he had known her grandmother or her progeny at all, he would have cut right to the chase. They were not a people given to tears and wailing, rarely in private and certainly not in settings like this. And besides, they had spent the past week entertaining a parade of well-meaning family and friends who had come to pay their respects after the funeral. Their glazed and silent repose was as much the result of an overdose of tuna casseroles as it was an exhaustion that inevitably and finally seized them.

"Well, then," he continued, extracting a pen from its velvet-lined case. "Let me proceed." He opened the folder. "This is the Last Will And Testament of Bernice Alberta Abernathy."

Amanda wondered why people adopted this particular affectation when speaking of important matters. The droning; the rhythmic lingering on and between words; the eye contact at regular intervals. She suddenly felt as if she had been hit by a blow dart. Her mother, who had not yet succumbed, elbowed her just as he broached the topic of bequeathing.

"To Iris Alexandra Abernathy, my only child, I give all my earthly belongings, excluding only those possessions which I bequeath to Amanda Eleanor Abernathy Forsyth, my only grandchild.

Mr. Crenshaw cleared his throat and continued. "The Yellow Bird bookstore, the farmhouse, the barn, and the property on which it stands, I bequeath to Amanda Eleanor Abernathy Forsyth on three conditions."

The word "bequeath" was starting to annoy Amanda, as was her grandmother's use of her formal name. Ungrateful as it sounds, this "farmhouse" Bernie had just "bequeathed" to Amanda had definitely seen better days, and by most people's standards wasn't even habitable. But it was a palace compared to the bookstore.

"The three conditions are as follows:

#1 Miss Forsyth must reside at my farm, beginning the first of the month following my death and must continue residing there for the following 12 months (or one year).

#2 During that year, Miss Forsyth shall be expected to sort through the deceased's belongings and determine their eventual fate.

#3. Miss Forsyth shall not sell, donate, or abandon the property or any of the deceased's books for the entire year. After the year has lapsed, she may do as she wishes."

"Oh great, she's given me a bookstore but I can't sell the books," Amanda said. "You know she's crazy, right?"

"There is a bit more," Mr. Crenshaw interjected. "Amanda will receive a monthly stipend for the year to cover the cost of carrying out my wishes."

"And if I don't carry out her wishes?"

"Then the property is to be sold and the proceeds are to go in full to her favorite charity."

"Which is?"

"The International Association for the Preservation of Books of Antiquity."

"Oh brother. And what about my mother? What does she get exactly?"

Mr. Crenshaw turned to her mother, "Do you care to explain, Mrs. Abernathy?"

Her mother coughed lightly and then told Amanda that while Bernie was not what one would call rich, she was certainly well-off, something she revealed to Amanda's mother only shortly before she died. Bernie also had asked her mother what it was that she wished for more than anything in the world. Her mother told Bernie she'd like to move to Chicago and start over – or start for the first time. Amanda realized that her mother's recent trip to Chicago wasn't only about selling medical supplies. She was also looking for a new home.

"That's what you want most of all, huh? A new home? I'll try not to take it personally."

"Amanda, think about it. I haven't been far from this New Jersey suburb since Bernie moved me up here to live with Aunt Lucy when I was a child. I grew up here, married here, divorced here, raised you here. Now it's my turn to see a little more of this world. Bernie has given me that chance. I told her that we should sell the farm and you could move to Chicago with me. But she refused. It was time for you to 'fly the coop,' is how she put it." Her mother stopped and looked down at her hands.

Amanda slumped in her chair. "Fly into the coop, she means. I don't like being told what to do, especially from the other side of the grave."

"It's up to you, Amanda. We can still sell the farm and give the money away. And you can either move in with me or somewhere else. I won't be renting the house much longer though."

"I know." Amanda already knew that she wasn't going to live with her mother if she could avoid it. Bernie was right about that. They both needed their own space.

"It's really up to you," her mother continued. "I've been nagging you about your plans for next year, or your lack of them. Now you're almost out of time. Think about it; most of your friends are away at college or headed there in the fall. What are you going to do? It's too late to apply to college."

"I know."

"So the way I see it, you have two choices. You can live with me and get a job or you can live for free at the farm while you sort things out. If you choose the farm, your dad will still be close enough to come down if you need help. Plus Chicago isn't that far if you want to visit or if you change your mind."

It sounded like a convincing argument, but Amanda knew better. This was coming from the very person who refused to step foot on the farm; her mother hadn't been there since she was a little girl. She said she was the urban-type at heart and had had more than her fair share of the back-to-nature experience, but Amanda didn't believe it. The truth was her mother was afraid of the place and Bernie knew it. Amanda, on the other hand, had been shipped off there whole summers at a time when she was younger, during the divorce and when her mother needed to go out of town. It was a weird place, but Amanda liked it all right, and overall her memories of it were happy ones.

"Okay, I'll try it. But contrary to Bernie's demands, I'm not making any promises. A year's a long time."

7

Amanda wanted to go by herself. At least the first time, or the first time since she was twelve. It was important for her to find her own way to the farm and reintroduce herself as an adult. Her mother understood and left her alone about it.

She packed everything she owned into the old blue Falcon station wagon (also a gift from Bernie) and headed down the turnpike through New Jersey and Delaware and took I95 past Washington and through Northern Virginia. She headed west through central Virginia and stopped for gas. The afternoon was good for traveling and she decided to abandon the interstate and drive the rest of the way on back roads. She relaxed into her seat and took in the warm September sunshine and cool breeze. Nothing but the scent of pine and forest blew in the windows. That and a little oil burning off the car's old engine block.

It was getting dark when she rolled into Porterstown and she was starving. She pulled up to the Silver Goose diner and was glad to see it was still open. Her grandmother always took her there for Sunday dinner where they'd get turkey melts and strawberry shakes. The outside was a little shabbier than she remembered. The blue and white metal awnings were sagging over the front windows and rust had chewed through the exterior in places. Amanda stepped inside and was instantly overcome by a scent that was hardwired to her memories. Twelve-year-old memories. The diner smelled sweet and salty all at once: coffee and bacon, donuts and ham, sundaes and fries. It smelled like Bernie.

"Help you?" asked an old lady behind the register.

"Just one for dinner," Amanda said.

"Sit anywhere you please," and she left to clear some tables.

Amanda sat at the counter. Everything seemed smaller than normal, like she was in a dollhouse. But she'd grown a lot since she was twelve, which would account for it. The broad mirror spanning the wall caught her off guard. All of a sudden, there she was, a stranger staring at herself. She stared back. So this is how she appeared to other people. Dark hair pulled into a thick ponytail, crazy wisps flying in every direction, defined brows planted over green eyes, a tan face, a little plain, a little smug, not much to distinguish her from a million other teenagers. Except that the arrangement of her features in the mirror somehow made her look older than she was.

The counter was the same pink and gold formica she remembered, and the red vinyl and chrome stools still swiveled. When Amanda was little, she used to twirl round and round on them spotting herself in the mirror on every pass, the way she had heard ballerinas did to keep from getting dizzy. This turned out to be a bad idea with a stomach full of milkshake. The same old jukebox stood in the corner and a man was feeding it with quarters. Ralph Stanley began "I've Always Been A Rambler" and it made her think of the summer Bernie's friend Gina showed her how to do the claw and hammer on the banjo. If only she'd paid more attention.

"What's your pleasure?" the old lady asked. She was stick thin, somewhere between fifty and sixty with platinum hair pinned into a French twist.

"Cheeseburger and fries."

As the waitress scratched down the order, Amanda watched a huge sapphire ring teeter on the woman's finger beneath a knob of knuckle. "Everything on it?"

"Except onions."

"Drink?"

"Just water, thanks."

She filled a glass with ice and held it under the tap. "You just passin' through?"

"Maybe. I'll be stopping by my grandmother's place for a little while. To check on things."

"Who's your grandma?"

"Bernie Abernathy. Did you know her?"

"Bernie? Good gracious, of course I know her, everybody around here knows her. When these folks aren't eatin' here you'd always find them at the Yellow Bird. At least you used to before she took ill. How's she holding up, honey?"

"Not too well. She died."

"Oh my." She set the coffee pot on the burner, leaned on the counter, and looked out the window. "I can't believe it," she said after a long silence. "She's gone, really gone. Oh my, I am so sorry. It's just so hard to believe. I knew how sick she was and in my mind I knew it was only a matter of time, but my heart? That's another matter altogether. I believed she'd be around forever. My oh my." She turned to Amanda again. "The last time I saw her was right over there at that booth. We sat and had a cup of coffee together. She said she was movin' in with her daughter and didn't think she'd be back. I told her that was nonsense, we'd have plenty more time for coffee. But, God bless her, she was right after all. That's a cryin' shame."

She disappeared into the kitchen and Amanda drank her water. The diner was about half full. Mostly old people. A few moms with their kids. Nobody her age as far as she could tell. Elvis crooned from the jukebox above the rumble of voices, dishes, and flatware. A soft pillowy sound rose up and fell away. It was coming from a plump bald man on the stool next to her and she realized finally that he was sobbing.

The waitress came back through the door leaving it swinging on its hinges. Her wet eyes were magnified through her glasses. "Virgil Lawson, get a hold of yourself," she barked at the man. "You cryin' like a baby ain't gonna bring her back. And it sure as hell ain't gonna help this young thing here." She pointed to Amanda. "Don't mind him, sweetheart, he's just missin' her already. That's a real shame, honey," she said, sliding Amanda's burger across the counter. "I'm so sorry. She was a prize, that one. Do you want ketchup?" She wiped off the top of the bottle and handed it to her. "And now here you are, Bernie's grandbaby. I don't believe I got your name. Mine's Mary Lynn."

"Amanda."

"That's right. Amanda. I do remember you. Didn't she bring you over here for supper from time to time? I thought so, and look at you, all growed up, and a beauty too." She tilted her head and grinned. "You've got a bit of her swimmin' around in that face. Mostly in the eyes, I think." Amanda could see she was holding back tears. "Makes me think about being young again. Those years when Bernie and I first met. It was really somethin'. We were a couple of wild things. Goodness gracious, just look at you. You know, Bernie was mighty proud of you. And that's no joke. She'd never have admitted it to you, of course," she poked Amanda's arm. "She never admitted to much of anything, but I knew better. She thought you were some kinda special. I can't believe she's gone. When did it happen?"

"About a month ago."

"Well folks around here were wonderin', 'cause she'd been so sick and all when she left and we hadn't heard. So you've come down to check on the farm?"

Amanda nodded.

"Good for you. That's the proper way to respect your elders, to look after their things after they pass. It's a comfort to know that the things in your life that held meaning are appreciated after you're gone. You're doin' right by her." She handed her the bill. "Now you let me know if you need help with anything, promise?"

8

Amanda decided to drive directly to the farmhouse and
deal with the bookstore later. It was dark by the time she reached
the house and a bright moon had crept up over the treed horizon.
It wasn't very late but she was exhausted anyway. She turned up the
gravel path and slowed to a crawl after she hit bottom on a piece of
the road that had washed away. As she reached the top of the hill, a
family of rabbits scattered in her headlights unaccustomed to any sort
of disturbance.

The old place shone blue in the moonlight. Amanda parked
in front of the wide porch and got out of the car. She should have
been afraid of this monster house, dark and alone and in the middle
of nowhere. Instead she felt comforted like it had been waiting for
her, like an old friend. She ran her hands along the rail at the top of
the steps feeling for her initials. There they were. AAF. She remembered scratching them into the hard wood when she was nine. She
walked across the porch, unlocked the door, and stepped inside. From
the small entryway, she could see silver light spilling in through
the windows and onto the living room floor. The house smelled of
mildew and dried grass. Like sage and damp rags, oil and lemons.
Bernie's reading chair was stationed just where she remembered it,
and its fat arms reached out of the shadows. Amanda turned on the

lamp next to it. The amber shade came alive and cast a warm glaze over the room. She saw the built-in bookshelves that devoured every wall from floor to ceiling and looking more laden than she remembered. Books, records, magazines, photographs, ornate boxes, rocks, shells, drawings, and notebooks. They filled every crevice and spilled onto the floor in places. A book lay open on the side table next to the chair. Amanda picked it up and turned it over: *The Physics and Evolution of Spirit in the Natural World.* She sat down and began reading where Bernie had left off.

Page 172: …their remarkably similar stories were recorded by Italian physicist Frederica Montaglio over the course of her fourteen years there. Montaglio explains the phenomenon in the April 1952 issue of *Science Today*:

"The elders with whom I studied are of a noble race, very sober in their opinions and careful in their descriptions of events, never given to hyperbole. The precision they employ through the spoken word is born out of necessity. They hold fast to a millennium-long oral tradition, passing knowledge from one generation to the next through their storytelling. Without a written language, a magnificent capability for memorization has evolved. They spend exceptional amounts of time reciting to their children with the expectation that the children will memorize the stories verbatim. A good deal of call and response is used to help them navigate the long and winding details of important historical events. Sometimes they use songs and poems to convey information as is the case, for instance, with many of their medicinal recipes, astronomical and nautical particulars, and the traditions of courtship and marriage.

"If a recitation requires parable or metaphor, as is often used in their morality plays, it will be commonly known or will be announced in advance if very young children are present. Otherwise accounts are considered to be literal. The following accounts describing Mabudago are of the latter tradition and therefore are very literal in the telling. The translation is my own."

The book dropped with a thud from Amanda's lap and she fell asleep. At least she thought she was sleeping; it was hard to tell. It felt like a waking dream or, more accurately, a waking nightmare.

First there was the hollow feeling. The sensation of falling asleep. Then there was a shrinking feeling. She was being pulled away from her skin, falling into a large cavern that was the middle of her body. She had become minuscule, an atom staring out of the black hole, a vortex, a crushing gravity. There, in that awful wasteland, she waited, afraid, terrified of something she couldn't name. Then it happened. Something entered her space, the space between her atom-self and her body. She didn't know what it was, but she knew it was bad and it was looking for her. She hid, or tried to but there was nowhere to go. Was this death? She didn't know.

There was no noise in this frightening world. No light either. Just emptiness. Vast dark void. Cosmic separation bubbling up between the cracks, the way lava eats through rock. She needed to stop it, plug up the holes, prevent the leaching of her soul by this now overpowering wickedness. But she couldn't stop it. She could only watch. There was nothing to be done. She suddenly understood that this was a condition of eternity, her eternity, and she felt herself relent and surrender and then she disappeared.

She woke up drenched in sweat and realized she had wet her pants. For chrissakes. All over Bernie's chair. And all her other clothes were still in the car. She felt as cold as ice from the dream and from the pee. What time was it? She stood by the window and saw a rim of pale light bleeding into the sky along the horizon. Morning must be near.

She walked out the front door and onto the porch. It smelled moist and new. The moon had set and all was dark except an orange triangle of lamplight spilling through the doorway, across the porch, and onto her feet. She stretched her limbs and rubbed her face. It had been almost three months since the accident and still the nightmares came. The doctors were hopeful that they'd subside in time. She wasn't so sure. She wondered how much time she had until they drove her completely crazy.

She walked around to the back of the car and tugged on the tailgate. Damn, stuck again. She kicked it twice and it opened. She pulled out her suitcases and dragged them into the house.

The kitchen was dark and she felt her way through to the bathroom on the other side. She pressed the black button on the wall that turned on the old florescent light and it crackled and popped until it lit the room. At least her mother had thought ahead and paid the electric bill. She lifted the lid on the toilet. Out of luck. No water and enough mold to choke a snake, which Amanda was pretty sure lived down there somewhere. Under the sink were the remnants of a mouse nest. The piles of droppings made her gag. She pulled open the shower curtain and it collapsed in the tub stained with rust and mold. Great, just great. She turned off the light and walked out.

The switch in the kitchen didn't work so she found a pack of matches and lit the kerosene lamp on the windowsill. The kitchen looked in better shape than the bathroom, but it was still dark outside and hard to tell. She tried the sink. The cold tap spewed dark rusty water. She turned it wide open and let it rip. The whole house sputtered and coughed and shook, belching the stagnant air from its pipes. She took off her pants and underwear and went outside to take a leak off the side of the porch. Back inside the water in the sink was running cool and clean. She pulled a washcloth out of her bag and held it under the faucet. She wrung it out and washed her crotch. How many seventeen-year-olds still wet their pants? She changed her clothes and sat on the porch until the sun came up.

9

The fiddler sawed out a lively reel for a small audience who listened beside the cotton candy machine. A clown approached on towering stilts wearing shiny red pants with more than a few conspicuous stains down the front. He waved his hat of stars and stripes at the children below who screamed and ran behind their mothers.

Cody worked the Dip-N-Win, which wasn't much but at least he could sit down when he needed to. The pay was lousy, but the job came with food and a bed, so he took it. He found he liked watching people, and traveling through these small mountain towns, he could watch an endless throng who had waited all year to make the pilgrimage to the carnival. People loved a good carnival, and they would tolerate a second-rate one, which this one was. But there was a good Ferris wheel and a passable Tilt-A-Whirl and so the people came. At first Cody didn't think of himself as a carny. After all, he was literate, and unlike most of the people in his family, he loved to read. Especially in the army when books became his only escape. Even in the hospital he managed to carry a small book of poems with him, something that earned him a good deal of ridicule.

But regardless of the taunts, he couldn't help but love words. In fact, he was addicted to them. The sound of them – all kinds of words. He had a particular fondness for the raw sounds that came out of the mouths of the carnies. They were unadulterated and pure. Unlike the words that came from the town's people – words that were whitewashed, sterilized, polished down to the shine, mirrors, a way for him to see himself the way they saw him. A glowering comment from a father who thought he looked a little too long at his Dip-N-Win daughter. The upstanding women of Glen Mills Methodist Church who went to magnificent lengths to make it appear that they had any interest in him whatsoever. They were there to do the Lord's work, after all. Yesterday he watched a mother shepherd her children clear to the opposite side of the tent just to avoid him altogether. It amused him and was a way to pass the day without lifting a finger.

"You going to let me play or not?"

Cody turned and saw a colored man holding up his ticket. He took it and the man said, "How do you play?" Cody pointed to the directions.

"Not going to get much business that way, young man. Look around you. That fellow at the ring toss is working the crowd, giving them a show. Just look at that line of people waiting to toss a few stinking rings for a chance to win big."

The man's quick smile somehow challenged Cody. "You wanna play or not?" Cody said and he lit up a cigarette.

"Okay, okay. I'll play. Where's the rod?" Cody lowered it from the ceiling. A line fed from the rod through a beam overhead and the hook dangled above a large blue cardboard tub filled with small stuffed animals, plastic squirt guns, and giant sunglasses.

"Here goes nothing," said the man. That smile again, innocent enough but the eyes went deeper; a dark brown that matched his skin.

"Got that right, mister," Cody found himself saying.

"Tomorrow, and tomorrow, and tomorrow," the man murmured, "creeps in this petty pace from day to day, to the last syllable of recorded time."

Cody laughed. "You ain't no Macbeth, mister. Hurry up. You're holding up the line."

The man slowly unwound the reel into the tub. "Life's but a walking shadow, a poor player that struts and frets his hour upon the stage and then is heard no more."

"A tale told by an idiot," Cody shot back. He took a long and easy drag and let the smoke drift between them.

The man raised an empty hook.

"Look, if it's mind games you want," Cody said, "you need to pay a visit to Madame Tootsweet at the Mystic Charms and Fortunes over there behind the House of Mirrors. She's never one to disappoint. I stake my reputation on it."

"I just might do that." He offered his hand and Cody shook it. "What's your name?" the man asked.

"Jeremiah."

"Stage name or real?"

"Real. What's yours?" Cody said blowing out an enormous cloud.

"I've been called lots of names. Lately it's been Reverend Joe, or Joe for short."

"Fair enough. And what brings you to this fine town, Mr. Joe? The scenery? The hallowed halls? The whores?"

"Revival. Tonight and Sunday. Quarter mile on this side of the Chalahume falls. Not too far from here."

"That's a little close to the white bread side of town, Rev. And I can tell you, they won't be sending you a welcome wagon, that's for sure, especially if you're inviting the likes of me."

"So you'll come?"

"Only if you got music."

"Do you play?"

"You'd be hard-pressed to find someone around here who can't play somethin'. What'd you need?"

"Guitar?"

"Okay. What time?"

"After you get off here."

"Mister, this place hasn't gotten me off in quite awhile. I do believe I'll be free to go whenever I please. I'll see you tonight."

He patted Cody on the back and disappeared into the crowd.

Cody sat on the stool and watched the crowd until they faded into the carnival's darkening landscape. The barker announced the next attraction through crackling speakers. Someone threw the switch and the lights came on. Cody closed his eyes against the bulbs that suddenly began to flash over the Dip-N-Win but they drilled through his lids anyway pulsing orange-red-orange-red. He could feel it coming on. His muscles tightened. A cold sweat broke across his forehead, a defense against the fire igniting in his brain. He pressed his palms over his sockets to fend off the attack. He shook his head, and then shook it again. He grabbed his guitar and left through the back gate.

10

The campfire flickered at the elbow of the Chalahume River where the slow dark water turned silently toward Porterstown about five miles downstream. He could hear the music rise up and linger over the camp. As he drew closer he could hear the singing. Not the thunder of black gospel he had expected, but the hard brittle hymns of mountain people. There were blankets spread out in places, where families sat eating and drinking. About fifty people in all. White people. Except for Joe and the woman sitting with him.

Joe spotted Cody standing on the edge of camp and he waved him down. "Jeremiah. I wasn't sure you'd show," Joe said when Cody approached, "Man, you look a little worse for the wear. What happened?"

Somewhere between the carnival and the camp Cody lost track of time. He still carried the chill that accompanied his attacks. It wasn't a bad one, compared to others he'd had. He still knew where he was when he came to, but the feeling was the same. Flashbacks, they called it, shellshock. Cody knew better. It had started out as flashbacks, reenactments of that night in the village. Same script but slowly distorted over time. The bodies were bodies at first, then they became something else, alive but not alive, a mass of limbs taking on a single form, a presence pressing itself into the dark recesses that had blown open in his mind after the explosion. An elusive but monstrous being looking for a place to inhabit, to possess. Cody had awakened flat on the ground in the woods sweaty and limp and feeling a little smaller inside. How long before he disappeared altogether?

"Come on, let's eat," Joe said, and he led Cody to the blanket where his wife was making sandwiches. "Martha, I'd like you to meet Jeremiah."

"Hello, Jeremiah," she said handing him a sandwich. "Hope you like ham."

"That'll do just fine."

"Not what you expected?" Joe asked.

"Not really. You're smart though. You wouldn't have lasted long out here by yourselves. It's still dangerous for the coloreds." Cody hadn't gotten used to seeing black families around these parts of Tennessee and Virginia. He knew how far civil rights had come. He saw it in the army where they drafted the poor, regardless of race. Being poor is what he and Clarence shared, it was their common ground. After the explosion, when they both had been shipped stateside, Clarence was the one who tracked him down in the hospital. And it was Clarence who stayed in his room for hours at a time, cracking stupid jokes to cheer him up, while they watched the riots break out on the nightly news too close to his home in Detroit.

Yet Cody also knew, that despite all that was happening in the world, little had changed in the hills along the Chalahume. Not just for blacks but for anyone who wasn't white and protestant. His mother still talked about Catholics as if they were from another planet.

"Yes, we know. But we have white friends in unexpected places and we don't mind asking for favors from time to time. What happened to you, Jeremiah?"

Cody wasn't used to being called Jeremiah, but he liked it. "Long story. I'm okay though. Who's the banjo picker?"

His name is Bill Jenkins. He's retired mostly, but he still works the railroad out of Winston now and then. You know him?"

Cody shook his head. "No, but he's good. Think he'd mind if I sat in?"

"On the contrary, he's been waiting for you."

Cody joined the cluster of musicians gathered at the bonfire. "You playin' any more tonight?" he asked them.

"You kiddin' me? We're just getting started," Bill said shaking Cody's hand. "Joe promised me a guitar player and I was beginning to wonder about the truth of his word. This here's my wife Anna who plays a mean streak on the accordion." Anna offered a little wave. "And brother Danny's keepin' time on bass."

"This ain't quite what I had in mind when Joe asked me to go on tour," Danny chuckled and he pushed his glasses back up his thick nose. "But I like it all right, though I don't mind saying I'm getting tired of haulin' this thing around," he patted his bass. "Should've taken up the harmonica or the flute. Tell you what, we'll let you play if you'll carry her back to the car afterwards."

Cody agreed and took his guitar out of the case.

Bill counted off the first tune, "Wayfaring Stranger," which Cody had been playing since he was a child. Bill and Danny ran through it a couple of times so he could get a feel for their way of doing it, then Anna joined in on the fourth round. She was a short middle-aged woman with jet black hair and snow white skin except along her check bones and throat where she was flush from the effort of her playing. She pumped the accordion slowly, drawing out its lower chords in mournful phrases that hummed beneath Bill's rapid picking. Danny began to sing and Bill stood up to add the top harmony with his sweet country tenor. When the next verse rolled around, he nodded at Cody inviting him to sing along. Cody did, taking up the bass line and filling out the sound with rhythm guitar. Anna came in next, a tense soprano, not shrill but not exactly pretty either.

When the song ended Bill wasted no time kicking off another. He led them into a rousing rendition of "This Little Heart of Mine." Cody watched as Bill worked the audience drawing them closer to the music with the pull of his good nature. Before long he had everyone singing along and wanting more. Anna stepped out front and began to buck dance. Others joined her. Soon the whole camp clapped and danced and brayed under the starry night in the warmth of the bonfire. The revival had begun.

They played "Gospel Ship," "I'm On My Way To Canaan's

Land," and "Wings Of A Dove". They finished with "The Angels Are Singing," and the crowd grew quiet. Reverend Joe stepped into the light of the fire and began his sermon.

Cody had never seen it done quite like this before. A black preacher with all these white folks attending to his every word. It made him nervous and he had trouble listening. But after a while he realized that Joe had taken the time to befriend every person there, the same way he had befriended him at the Dip-N-Win. That's what made it work. He knew these people and they knew him. He spoke to their troubles, their loss, their impossibilities. He made them feel like their problems mattered, he made them feel better, made them believe that things would get better. He told his own story, the times when his life was broken, when he had given up hope. He talked about how life was still hard, but how now he lived it with joy, a joy that dwelled within him the moment he asked for it. It had changed his life. It didn't take courage, he told them. It took having nowhere else to go. Who would ask today? Who among you has reached the end? Who among you will ask to be filled with the Holy Spirit, the sacred and eternal spirit of the living God?

Cody suddenly felt embarrassed by the intimacy that had captivated the moment. He liked being on the edge of things looking in, and this was a little too close. Joe glanced at the band and smiled at Cody. Bill counted off the next tune soft and slow: "Just As I Am" and the rest of the band followed suit, except for Cody who sat down and lit a cigarette.

Reverend Joe stood silently, head bowed in prayer and he waited. An old lady with rheumy legs crept forward holding onto the arm of her son. Joe held out his hand and she grasped it. A teenage boy with a crop of red hair and an overbite came next, then two women who appeared to be sisters. A couple who held a newborn baby. A man in a suit, a woman in a housedress. They all held hands and prayed together, quietly, undisturbed by the popping fire, by the slapping of the river on its rocky banks, by the rise and fall of the locusts calling from the shivering night. In silence they stood, eyes closed and faces open. "Hallelujah and amen," Joe whispered. He told them to expect a change. From here on out, the fabric of their soul would be different. He invited them to return the following evening, to share their testimonies and to be baptized if they desired it.

Again he signaled the band and Bill started plucking "Amazing Grace." Cody played it too. People began to gather their things. Two men in overalls filled buckets and doused the fire sending a column of blue steam into the sky. Soon the crowd thinned to the last car that started up and drove off. Joe walked up and thanked Bill and gave Anna a peck on the cheek. He walked over to Danny and hugged him. Then he turned to Cody and smiled. "So what'd you think?"

Cody shrugged, "You put on a good show, Rev."

"Glad you approve. Will you come back tomorrow? That guitar sounds awfully good."

"I'll think about it. Right now I've got to keep a promise." He picked up Danny's bass and started toward the parking lot.

"Where you staying?" Joe called after him.

"Tonight? I've got a room back near the carnival. My job comes with benefits."

"You'll be all right, then?"

"What are you, my mother? Yeah, I'll be fine. Danny can drop me off."

"Okay, try and make it tomorrow," and he walked over to where Martha stood waiting for him.

11

I t was midnight by the time Cody crept into his room in the trailer behind the Mystic Charms and Fortunes. He could hear Marlene snoring from the next room. He wasn't sure if she had a man with her tonight. He didn't want to know. He threw himself on the bed and stared at the ceiling. He was exhausted and wired all at once and his leg was killing him. He looked out at the trailer across the way to see if Penny was still up; maybe she'd front him a couple of pills again. Her light was on so he figured it was worth a try.

Penny was nice enough when she was sober, but lately more often than not she was either drunk or strung out. Cody never knew which Penny he'd encounter, the angel or the devil, which is why he tapped gingerly on her front door. When no one answered, he tried again. He thought he heard voices so he cracked the door and looked inside. Penny was passed out on the couch, still in the purple-sequin gown and feathered turban she wore when she read palms. Her pink pancake makeup had melted into the creases of her face and black mascara ran from the corners of her eyes.

Then he heard someone crying. It came from the bedroom. Cody crept back through the narrow hall and listened. "Karla, you in there?" he asked. Karla, Penny's fourteen-year-old daughter, had lately taken to following Cody around whenever she could, flirting shamelessly. She was tall and smooth and beautiful, but even Cody knew when to leave well enough alone. She was still a child after all. Jailbait.

"Karla?" He opened the door. Karla sat naked on the bed with her arms wrapped around her legs, knees pulled tightly to her chest. She rocked back and forth and sobbed. "Karla!" The words barely left his mouth when Cody felt a hard thud between his shoulder blades and he hit the floor. Karla screamed. He turned just in time to see a fat man clamber toward the door with his pants thrown over his arms. Cody grabbed him by the ankle and the man stumbled, giving Cody enough time to draw his knife and thrust it. The man howled and barreled out the door into the night.

"Holy shit!" Cody said running his hands through his hair. "Who the hell was that?" Karla turned away and stared blankly at the wall. Cody sat on the bed, "Karla!" He shook her. " Did he touch you?" She shook her head, no. "Are you telling me the truth? Answer me!" Yes, at least Cody had gotten there before that. Karla mumbled something into the pillow. "What? Say it again."

"He's coming back," she told him. "He said if anyone found out, he'd come back, finish the job, and then kill me."

"Jesus Christ. Put on your clothes." He gathered what he could find of them on the floor and threw them at her. "We're getting out of here. Hurry up."

She put on her t-shirt and jeans, "What about Mama?"

"What about her?"

"What if he comes back and finds her? What if he kills her?"

"Your mama can take care of herself. She always has. It's you she's had trouble taking care of. She's got no business turning tricks with a child to look after. That man is a marshmallow drone if I ever saw one, just out for a good time. Hardly a cold-blooded killer. But you're a witness and underage and no tellin' what a man will do when pushed into a corner. Come on. Let's go."

12

Amanda woke with the sun on her face. Either it had rained or the dew was extra thick on the grass. Droplets formed along the telephone wires and she watched them collect the morning light until they burst from the weight of their own brightness and shower to the ground, a mist of broken color.

She could hear the soft moaning of Mr. Greer's cows in the distance, waiting to be milked. A tractor grumbled further off, Mr. Greer or maybe one of his sons was already out in the fields cutting hay along the field that adjoined the Yellow Bird on the north side.

A large speckled chicken flew onto the porch and it made Amanda jump. In one deft move the hen speared a cricket that leaped along the planks. Unaccustomed to human company, the hen eyed Amanda suspiciously while the cricket wriggled in her clamped beak.

"Hey there, love," Amanda said. "You think *that's* good, I got a couple of mice I'd like you to meet," and the hen fluttered off toward the barn.

She rubbed her forehead. A caffeine headache was starting behind her eyes, but she'd hold off on making coffee; it was still too early to face the mess that waited for her inside. Out here everything smelled clean and new and she wanted to make it last.

She walked around to the back of the house and the view stopped her in her tracks. From here she could see the whole thing. Her grandmother's farm, her farm now. The towering bank barn across a wide drive. Gnarled cedars in straight lines marking boundaries. Further up, on a steep hill was the bookstore.

A morning fog hovered above a glinting stream that wound over the pastures and wooded acres sloping toward the gap. It was good lowland soil, Bernie used to say. Beyond it, the Chalahume River cut through a deep gorge. Its granite banks on the opposite side soared a hundred feet high to a plateau where the railroad passed. It was beautiful. But even abandoned fields look good this time of day. She sat down in the long wet grass.

She had a year to figure it out. What to do. How to do it. The remnants of a kitchen garden lingered in the plot closest to the house. The weeds had taken over. A tangle of honeysuckle and bindweed sprawled over the deer fence where it had fallen down on one side. A farm looks romantic until you think about working it. Now in the increasing strength of the sun, everything looked a little desperate.

Maybe she'd just let the whole thing grow over and forget about it. Bernie never made any money off it anyway, as far as she knew. Except the times she rented out a parcel or two when the Greers needed more room to graze their Guernseys.

The sun began to feel hot, so she brushed herself off and walked back to the car. Her mother had helped her pack some groceries to tide her over until she could get to the store. She found the ground coffee and sugar but they forgot to pack cream.

The sun that drenched the earth outside did not find entry into the house easily. Even in the dazzling light of late morning, the shade trees and the roof over the porch lent a cave-like aspect to the living room. A generous layer of dust covered everything, except the places where Amanda had trod to and from Bernie's chair the night before. She walked straight through to the kitchen, which was brighter but not any cleaner. This kind of grime didn't happen overnight.

Bernie must have given up on cleaning a long time ago. Amanda knocked down the cobwebs in the cabinet over the stove and grabbed the old percolator from its rightful place. She rinsed it off, filled it up with water, and scooped the grinds into the metal basket. The socket next to the sink looked sketchy but she plugged it in anyway. And waited. And waited. *Kerplop plop plop kerplop.* At last.

After her third cup, she braced herself for the inevitable: the examination of the refrigerator. It was closed tight and it was unplugged, a bad combination. What was Bernie thinking? She held her nose and pulled. Better than she expected; Bernie must have emptied it before she left and only a healthy growth of black mold remained. Amanda plugged it in and it lit up. Another victory. Time to start cleaning before her luck changed.

She turned on the hot water faucet and soon steam began to rise from the sink. Another good sign. She found a pail, filled it with hot soapy water and bleach, and attacked the refrigerator. With renewed resolve and determination and a steady dose of caffeine, Amanda tore through the kitchen, ceiling to floor, and was finished by late in the afternoon. She sat at the cracked but spotless laminate table and ate bologna sandwiches while contemplating the way the old fridge reminded her of a 1950 Buick.

By nightfall, Amanda had tackled enough of the living room and bedroom to shield herself against the marauding bacteria she imagined would crawl over her in the dark. She fell into Bernie's armchair exhausted and picked up *The Physics and Evolution of Spirit in the Natural World,* which was lying face down on the floor where she dropped it the night before.

"…. The following accounts describing Mabudago are of the latter tradition and therefore are very literal in the telling. The translation is my own."

A young couple had a son who became increasingly troubled by night terrors. They brought their son to the village shaman who asked the boy to describe his dreams. The boy could not speak, so fearful was he of the dream and the power he believed it held over him. The shaman asked the boy if he was able to nod yes or no to questions. The boy nodded yes.

"Each time your dream begins, do you find yourself in the same place or situation?"

The boy thought it over carefully. Yes.

"Does the dream change as it progresses?"

Yes.

"How? Does the place change?"

He shrugged.

"Do the people change?"

Yes, and he tapped his chest.

"Do you change?"

Yes.

"How?"

He spread out his arms and then drew them close until his hands touched.

"Do you grow smaller and smaller?"

The boy covered his eyes and tried to make the shaman stop.

"Is it dark?"

The boy began to shake.

"Is it alive?"

The boy's eyes grew wide and then he fell to the ground motionless. His parents ran to him weeping, fearing he was dead.

"Do not be alarmed," advised the shaman, "He is only sleeping. Bring him to me."

The father lifted the lifeless boy and delivered him to the shaman's arms.

"Mabudago has made a home inside your son," he said. "Fear not, Mabudago can only inhabit empty spaces. Your son must be filled to drive out the intruder."

His mother asked how this could be accomplished.

"You do it," he said to her.

The shaman placed the woman's hand on her son's heart. "Do you believe?" he asked her. Yes, the woman nodded. "Let it be as you believe."

The boy awoke and began speaking to his parents. With great joy he told them of the marvels and wonders he had witnessed while asleep. "He is healed," the woman told the shaman.

"Yes," said the shaman, and as he delivered the boy to his parents, he admonished them, "Feed him."

13

Cody woke up with the sun already high over the trees. He and Karla had spent the night in the woods where he was pretty sure no one would find them. His leg was numb but it wasn't throbbing as much as it had during the night. Karla looked even younger asleep, he thought, too young for the kind of trouble she was in. He walked behind some bushes and peed. It must be noon already.

Karla jumped when he came back up the hill but relaxed when she saw it was Cody. "I thought maybe you'd gone and left me here to fend for myself," she said.

"No such luck," he said lighting up a smoke.

"Now what?" she asked.

Cody shrugged.

"Well I'm starving. Did you bring anything to eat?"

"Right, like I filled my pockets on the way out last night."

"I gotta eat or I'll faint."

He ran his fingers through his hair. "I think there's a Mighty Mart down the road about a mile. You up for a hike?"

"Got nothin' else to do except piss. You go ahead. I'll catch up with you in a minute."

He found a sturdy stick on the ground and tried it out. It made a passable cane and he started down the hill that led toward town.

In hindsight, Cody wished they had spent a little more time grooming before they ventured into the store. The ultra-shiny floors and bright lights made him feel conspicuous and even grimier than he was, and he was pretty pungent just about now. He picked a leaf out of Karla's hair and brushed the litter off her back. She looked at him adoringly and tried to hold his hand.

He pulled away. "Stop it, Karla." She pouted and began to browse through a rack of nail polish. "And I'm not your babysitter either. Put that down. Let's get something to eat and get out of here."

They moved quickly through the express line, but when the cashier handed Cody his change, she spent a little too long looking them over.

"What are you staring at?" Karla snarled.

"Not a thing, darlin'," she said, handing her the bag. "I think it's kinda sweet to see a brother and sister out getting the groceries." Cody got the sarcasm; Karla did not.

"Let's go," he said.

They hiked back up the long trail and then followed the river to a clearing in the woods. Karla cracked open the peanut butter and ate it right out of the jar.

Cody pulled out the bread and Velveeta. "Thirsty?" he said tossing her a Coke.

"Yeah, and gimme the chocolate too."

Cody lit up and stretched out on the ground trying not to think.

"Are you taking me home tonight?" she asked licking her fingers.

"No."

"But Mama's gotta be worried sick by now. I have to let her know that I'm okay."

"Yeah I know. But you can't go back just yet, not after what happened last night. We'll figure somethin' out." He stamped out his cigarette. "Come on."

"Where we goin'?" She ran to catch up before he disappeared over the hill.

14

Joe saw Cody and Karla as soon as they emerged from the woods at the back of the campground. He had been waiting for them. It was too early for the revival and no one but Joe, Martha, Bill, and Anna had arrived yet.

As they approached, he asked, "Are you all right?"

"Yeah, why?"

"And this must be Karla."

"How'd you know that?"

"Because you've got the Porterstown authorities asking about you two. Someone saw you leave with her last night and they notified the police."

Cody sat on the ground and pressed his hands over his eyes.

"Hello, Jeremiah," Martha said. "Joe, can I help out here?"

"Karla, will you go with Martha for a little while?" Joe asked. "I need to talk to Jeremiah alone."

"Jeremiah? Who the hell is Jeremiah? Is she going to hand me over to the cops, Cody?"

"That'd be a whole lot better than you goin' home right now." Cody said. "But you're in a mess either way. Ain't that right Rev?"

"Karla," Martha said, "we're just going to sit with Anna and Bill over there by the riverbank so Jeremiah and Joe can talk. Is that all right with you?"

Karla looked at Cody for an answer but he just stared at the ground. "I suppose so," she said finally and they walked off.

"They say it's statutory rape," Joe told Cody, "and they're waiting for you in the parking lot."

He looked up at Joe, "What'd you tell 'em?"

"I told them that I could vouch that you were here last night, which was the truth."

"So what do you think happened?"

"I don't *know* what happened. That's why I was trying to find you before they did. So you could tell me. Here's your chance. You only have a few minutes."

"And then what?"

"Then it's up to you. I want to help you if I can but you need to tell me the truth. Sooner or later you'll have to face the police. I can tell you, though, it'd be better for you if you did it sooner rather than later."

Cody laid on the ground. "You can't send her back home."

"Why not."

"Just don't. It's not safe for her there. I brought her here so you could look after her for a while. Ain't that what preachers do? Shepherd the sheep and all that? Or do they just bow to the police 'cause it's easy?"

"Did you touch her?"

Cody bristled. "Well, Rev, I can see now how highly you must think of me to ask that."

"You didn't answer the question."

Cody stared at Joe and felt his soul freeze over. "I don't have to answer anything or anybody. And I don't intend to. Especially you since it's clear you've already made up your mind about me. Draw your own damn conclusions." He pulled himself up off the ground and winced at the pain shooting up his leg. "Thanks for the endorsement, Rev." He limped down the hill, through the trees, and into the parking lot where the police were waiting for him.

15

Someone was shaking her. "Amanda, wake up. What's wrong with you? Wake up!"

It was Dehlia. "How long have you been asleep in that chair?"

"I don't know. What time is it?"

"About eleven."

"In the morning?"

"Of course, stupid. That would account for the sunshine. It took me a long time to wake you up. Were you having one of your epipeptic seizures?"

"Epileptic. No it's not that. Just a bad dream. What are you doing here?"

"Your mom's been trying to call you from Chicago but your phone's out. So she called me and asked if I'd drive down to check on you. I got lost twice. Once getting off of 81 in Virginia and then trying to find the farm after I got through Twin Gap. I completely overshot the driveway. Your neighbor on the other side showed me how to get here. Man, you were really out of it. If I didn't show up when I did, you might have stayed unconscious for days and days and starved to death or something."

"I think I was just tired. I'm fine, really. Now that you're here, though, you going to stay over?"

"Of course. It's Labor Day weekend and I don't have to be back on campus until Tuesday. Freshman year stinks."

"I thought it'd be a breeze since you were such an egghead in high school." Amanda said.

"Well it's not. My roommate's a Barbie doll and my medieval lit professor is a monster," she sniffed. "So am I going to spend the day standing here staring at you or are you going to get up and show me around?"

"You hungry?" Amanda asked and she led her into the kitchen.

Dehlia opened the refrigerator and tallied up the possibilities which were slim at best.

On their way to the grocery store, Dehlia asked, "So how are you going to pay for food anyway or anything else for that matter? Is your mom sending you money?"

"No but my grandmother left me some in an account in town. We need to stop by there first, and I need gas, too. And there's a phone booth at the diner so remind me to call my mom while we're there."

"You should buy a new car," Dehlia decided.

"She didn't leave me *that* much money."

The Mighty Mart was having its Labor Day sale, and even on Sunday, it drew throngs from as far away as Bristol. After getting nearly trampled at the dairy section, they headed down the aisle for some cereal.

"You want to get Cocoa Puffs?" Dehlia asked lifting a box off the shelf. "I've had these in the dining hall and they're scrumptious. What'ya think, Amanda. Amanda?"

Amanda stood by the pancake mix starring at the floor. "Amanda." Dehlia grabbed her arm.

Amanda pulled away and shook her head. She suddenly felt like she was falling down a tunnel. Her head began to throb and she thought she might faint. If she could just hang on a few more minutes it was likely to pass. Dehlia sensed she was in trouble and stood next to Amanda to keep her from getting run over by the carts barreling down the aisle vying for position. Through the ringing in her ears, Amanda could hear Dehlia rambling on the way she did when she was nervous. "You wouldn't believe what they put in food these days. It's just dreadful. What the hell is calcium benzoate anyway?"

"I've been there before," Amanda told Dehlia on their way back to the farm.

"When?"

"Never. I mean I've never been in the Mighty Mart but I suddenly knew all about it, like I'd been up and down those aisles before."

"So what? It's probably ESP or something. Or maybe Bernie brought you there when you were a kid."

"It wasn't even built back then. No, it's something else." Amanda didn't say anymore and Dehlia didn't ask. What Amanda didn't say is that she had been there, but with someone else, through someone else. She had been there with him yesterday while she slept in Bernie's chair.

"So now what do you want to do?" Dehlia asked as they unpacked the groceries.

"I was going to tackle the living room next," Amanda said. "You feel like cleaning?"

Dehlia bit into an apple, "Nope, what else you got."

"I haven't been to the bookstore yet. I've got no idea what we'll find over there."

"Perfect. Let's go."

"All right. If I remember correctly, we can get there through the back door past the barn down a little lane. It's up the hill on the left."

"Okay but sounds like we'll be needing reinforcements," Dehlia said grabbing a bag of Fritos and some dip.

The path to the barn was still visible where it had been laid years ago, but the gravel had long since sunk beneath a thick layer of moss-covered clay. On either side, timothy and alfalfa grew waist high. On their right a narrow field stretched out to the road; on their left was the old gray bank barn that smelled of rotting wood and cool dank earth. They entered the barn on the second floor through two broad sliding doors that groaned when they opened them. Swallows dove and swooped and mice ran for cover in the matted straw. Amanda and Dehlia stepped into the haymow overlooking a number of stalls on the ground floor fifty feet below them. The high walls were vented with dozens of small slatted windows that bent the sunlight into strange patterns. Above them, enormous hewn rafters reached overhead and they could see families of small bats sleeping along the trusses.

"Let's keep going," Dehlia said backing up. "This place makes me timorous, especially those bats."

"Timorous?" Amanda laughed, latching the doors behind them.

"You know what I mean. Besides, I want to see the bookstore."

They continued up the path until they reached a clearing in the canopy of trees. Amanda looked one way and then the other and then crouched to inspect the ground for signs of the brick lane. "I can't find it," she said. "It doesn't matter, though, the store's just on the other side of those hedge rows."

Amanda strode into the thicket using her arms to clear the way and Dehlia followed close behind. They came to the place where an unbridled rush of roses stretched over the arch of an old stone gate, an impenetrable fortress of bloomless thorns. They slogged their way down the length of the hedge avoiding the barbs and pricks as best they could. Finally they came to a break and they climbed through. Amanda saw it first – the old yellow clapboard bookstore.

"It's beautiful," Dehlia whispered.

They found the remnants of the brick path emerging from the shade of a small copse of arthritic apple trees and they crossed over the lawn to where a spacious patio of blue and gray stone abutted the back of the store.

A massive oak table stood in the middle of the patio flanked on either side by long worn benches. A mildewed awning hung over the backdoor and a faded sign dangled by a single nail – Y E L L O W   B I R D.

"Is this the way you remember it?" Dehlia asked.

"Sort of. Bernie and I had picnics out here a lot. She loved this spot. Only she had all kinds of great smelling herbs and mounds of flowers all around that wall. Now look at it. Nothing but weeds the size of dinosaurs." Amanda ran her hand over the wall's cool surface. "Watch this," she said. She slipped her hand into a deep notch and pulled out an iron key.

"You and I are now the only living souls who know where this key is hidden," she said. "You are hereby sworn to secrecy." They walked over to the back door and Amanda pushed the key into the rusty and reluctant lock. It whined and grunted as she tried to turn it and finally it popped open.

The smell of worn wood, old books, and chimney smoke inundated her senses. The store was unchanged and she felt twelve years old again. There in the backroom were the small stove and sink with the wooden cabinets above them. On the other side were the neatly made cot with the red and white pinwheel quilt folded at the foot, and the door to the little bathroom. Everything looked fresh and lived in. Bernie must have spent most of her time here toward the end, Amanda thought. A narrow passage led to the storefront, a long room with books floor to ceiling along the walls as well as on stacks that ran down the center. A wooden stairway was on their left, which opened to an attic loft where Amanda often slept when she and Bernie stayed up too late playing cards on the patio. In the front of the store at the bottom of the stairs was a windowed alcove with two overstuffed chairs around a small round table. An old crank register sat on a glass counter on the other side of the front door.

"Wow," Dehlia whispered as if she were in a museum. "Why didn't you take me with you on those summer trips? This is amazing."

"Because after my mother described the farm and Bernie to your mother, she wouldn't let you go."

"Oh yeah, that's right. That was when I found myself suddenly enrolled in summer camp."

As the afternoon rolled on, the sun flooded the alcove where Amanda and Dehlia relaxed in the plush chairs. Children's books, magazines, old encyclopedias, romance novels, ornate books of poetry, and cookbooks lay in piles on the table and in their laps. Dehlia snored softly while Amanda leafed through a small leather-bound collection of *The Apocryphal Acts*. There was something about "The Acts of Paul and Thecla" that grabbed her attention and she read halfway through before waking up Dehlia.

"Wake up and check this out," Amanda said. "You ever hear of Thecla?"

"Is it some sort of disease?" Dehlia guessed rubbing her eyes.

"No. Thecla's a person. A woman from the second century who was an aristocrat from a city called Iconium and engaged to one of the big shots there. According to the story, the apostle Paul came to town and began preaching in the streets. Thecla listened to him from her window and once she heard him talk she was converted."

"Let me guess, her betrothed didn't take it too well."

"It gets worse. Paul preached that the way to heaven, among other things, was through virginity and all the women thought that was great and were flocking to hear him. It got so bad that a lot of the wives began refusing to have sex with their husbands. That's when the real trouble started. Especially for Thecla whose well-connected beau would not be made a fool and so he got Paul thrown in jail. But Thecla converted anyway and she snuck out of her house in the dark of night to find Paul. She got into his cell by bribing the guards with her jewelry."

"That's kind of romantic, in an odd sort of way."

"It says that her faith was affirmed when she saw that 'by divine assistance' Paul wasn't afraid of what might happen to him. Eventually her fiancé found her and brought her to trial before the governor. When she still refused to marry him, her mother stood and began to shout." Amanda jumped up on the chair and started shaking her fist. "'Let the unjust creature be burned; let her be burned in the midst of the theater for refusing Thamyris, so all women may learn from her to avoid such practices.'"

Dehlia sat up in her chair, "Whoa, now that's a screwed up family."

"Yeah, it gets better. They bring her naked to the amphitheater and lay up a huge bonfire. Then the crowd commands her to walk into the middle. When she does, it mentions that the governor 'was surprised to see the greatness of her beauty.' An interesting aside, don't you think? Anyway, they light the fire and the flames roar up. Thecla is untouched by the fire and an earthquake and hailstorm put it out. She leaves the amphitheater unscathed."

"Thecla, Super Virgin!"

"Then she goes to Antioch and beats up a magistrate who tries to kiss her. Naturally, he sends her into an arena with a bunch of wild animals, wherein Thecla decides, 'Now is a proper time for me to be baptized,' and she throws herself into the shark-infested pool." Amanda plunged back into the chair. "After she baptizes herself, lightening and fire explode all over the place and all the sharks float to the top dead. Then she's surrounded by a cloud of fire that protects her from the wild beasts and also 'so the people could not see her nakedness.'"

Amanda closed the book, "It goes on, but what a story."

"I never could figure out what's with the whole celibacy thing. Do you think there's anything to it? I mean, that virgins have a special place in heaven?"

"I sure hope not or else heaven's got to be a real lonesome place."

16

How long had he slept? He wasn't sure. Cody looked at his watch. It was four-thirty in the afternoon. Which meant it was Monday. His jail cell was small and smelled awful. Or maybe he smelled awful. He hadn't had a shower since who knows when.

He could tolerate being locked up. Not a whole lot different than the barracks, only here he had the advantage of being alone. The walls were old and cracked and he could hear a man crying somewhere across the hall. He began to remember all that happened to him since the night before: the reverend, the cops, his refusal to speak, his arrest. Somewhere along the way he had climbed over the edge. His fragile lifeline to sanity had snapped and now he was adrift in his own body. Nothing mattered now, not even jail.

Except there was the dream. The one he woke from just now. The dream mattered. It wasn't the usual kind, the terrifying nightmares that left him shaking when he woke. And it wasn't the blank gray void that passed for sleeping more often than not. No, this dream was different. He could still feel it. It was real. He had been there.

He dreamed he was sitting in an overgrown lawn next to an old storefront window. He heard someone speaking, her voice so clear. Now she shouted, her words taking on form. The form of a woman, unclothed and poised on top of a pyre. She was so young and yet so unafraid of the violent and contorted horde howling and jeering as they lit the fire beneath her. He watched as the flames climbed up around her, the sweat on her lithe body, the flush of her face, the tension in her jaw, her utter lack of fear. He reached out to touch her and the flames fell away into swirling eddies around her feet.

The woman turned and looked at Cody. "Come near," she said, holding out her hand. He stepped into the water that gathered and spun, rising up and up. She opened her palm and he saw a pool of white light. She tipped her hand and poured the glinting water over his leg. "You shall be fulfilled this day," she said. Then she threw herself into the river.

Cody heard footsteps approaching from down the hall. The deputy sheriff appeared and removed the set of keys from his belt loop. He unlocked the cell door. "Let's go," he said motioning to Cody. When Cody stood, a shock ran through the long scar on his thigh and he yelped. "What's the matter, boy?" the deputy asked. Cody shrugged and shook his leg. It was stiff but not sore. A tingling sensation ran all the way up through his spine and down again. The pain was gone. He followed the deputy out the door.

17

"Rev can tell it better," Danny told Cody as they got in the car. "He said all the charges were dropped and asked if I could come get you. But I think they released you 'cause you stink so bad. Man, when's the last time you had a bath?" Danny pulled out of the parking lot and onto the highway.

"Where we goin'?"

"Up to Winston to Bill and Anna's house. Rev and Martha are over there waitin' for you." When Cody was silent, Danny added, "You know who I mean? Bill and Anna, Jenkins Country Band, the Reverend Joe and his wife from the revival?"

"For chrissakes, Danny. I know who they are. I just want to know why you're takin' me there. Joe's the last person I want to see right now."

"Well that's a poor state of mind considering he's the one who saved your sorry ass," Danny said with a wide grin. With one hand on the wheel, Danny began his monologue about all that had transpired since the day before. Cody learned that Joe "went into action as soon as you was arrested." Joe, he found out, was a lawyer as well as a preacher, and he managed to "get to the heart of the matter before the rest of us knew what was going on." Cody was relieved when they reached Winston, not so much by all he had learned about Joe, but because their arrival caused Danny to finally stop talking long enough to draw a breath. They drove to the other side of town to where the Jenkins house stood at the top of a long gravel lane.

Bill greeted them at the door and he slapped Cody on the back. "Glad you could make it, young man," he said and he led them into the living room. Anna and Martha rushed up and hugged him. Joe shook his hand and smiled. "Have a seat."

"Hold it right there," Anna interjected. "I think your business can wait for Jeremiah to wash up and have somethin' to eat. Lord knows the last time he had a decent meal. Come on, Jeremiah, the bathroom's over there, and the clean towels are in the cabinet next to the sink. Bill, why don't you show him where everything is and while you're at it see if you've got a spare set of clothes that'll fit him. I've got supper to look after," and she disappeared into the kitchen.

Bill shrugged. "What can I say? She runs a tight ship," and Cody followed him down the hall.

Cody's stomach ached when they gathered around the table piled high with fried chicken, mashed potatoes, gravy, and greens. He was way beyond hungry, and he wasn't sure if he could keep any of it down. Everyone bowed their heads when Joe gave the blessing and, with his eyes closed, Cody's dream brightened in his mind. He ate slowly at first and before long he was ravenous. "It's nice to see a young man with a hearty appetite," Anna said.

"Thank you, ma'am," Cody said. "I'm much obliged."

After supper, Cody and Joe sat out on the back porch. The fire-flies were long gone leaving the night to the sirens of cicadas.

"Why'd you do it?" Cody asked.

"Because I said I would."

"I didn't believe you, you know. I thought I had you figured out." Cody saw Bill's guitar in the corner. "Mind if I play some? It helps me think." He pulled it off the stand, tucked it under his arm and started picking. "So how'd you get me out?" he said finally.

Joe told him the whole story. About how Martha was able to cajole Karla into telling her what had happened. It wasn't the first time that man had been around their trailer. He was one of Penny's regulars, and when Penny passed out, he thought he'd pay Karla a visit. There were no witnesses among the people in the trailer park, the man made sure of that, and he'd been careful in his comings and goings so her description alone wasn't enough to identify him.

"Then Karla remembered something," Joe continued. "She said that when you came into her room that night, the man struck you from behind and knocked you down. 'When he tried to run off,'" Joe said imitating Karla, "'Cody pulled a knife, grabbed his leg, and cut him clean across his fat ass'." Finally, Cody cracked a smile. "So we searched the hospitals for patients with this particular affliction. Sure enough, there was a man in Glenn Mills General who claimed to have fallen on a shard of glass after he accidentally broke a mirror."

"That's bad luck," Cody said.

"His name is Roy Braxton, Councilman Braxton, to be precise. Upstanding fellow with a fine reputation. Happens to also sit on the board of Winston Coal & Fuel, although I imagine he won't be sitting anytime soon. We've had a little chat with the councilman, who for some unknown reason is very eager to settle matters out of court. He received twenty-two stitches. That's impressive, Jeremiah."

"So he's getting away with it, huh?"

"Not at all. Either in court or out, he'll pay. He's already resigned from the town council, which is just the beginning. We'll make sure the consequences of his actions are fully satisfied."

"What about Karla?"

"Martha is working with social services. Right now she's staying with an aunt in Twin Gap. And her mother's little side show has been shut down."

Cody kept strumming the guitar. No moon tonight but the stars were magnificent. "Can I ask you something?"

"What?"

"Do you believe in angels?" he asked.

Joe looked at him. "Sometimes, why?"

"You ever see one?"

"Can't say that I have, no."

"Would you believe 'em if you did?"

"I'd like to think so."

He stopped playing and faced Joe. "Then I want you to take me down to the river."

"Now?"

"Now."

Book Two

Mirror mirror on the wall
How can you claim to see it all
A downy wing, a dying breath
The places where souls lay to rest

Legends steeped in dust and brine
Forgotten to the sands of time
Buried on the hidden shores
Where pounding waves guard all the doors

When ages break upon the stones
And wisdom waits for ends unknown
And birthing pains roll up the scroll
And blind men say I didn't know

The moon is up
The air is still
Who will come and steal the till
Her silver beacon on the tide
Revealing where the sinners lie
Where mysteries keep their secrets well
The story whispers never tell

The world spins cold and circles round
The promises released unbound
When hands of angels consecrate
The farthest reaching glory gate

And down upon the misty shore
When voices sing no more no more
The day has come, make haste make haste
The looking glass is laid to waste

18

What was that? She could hear people singing. No. They were birds. The way they sound in the late afternoon, when the sun has rolled back toward South Mountain, and the cardinal takes the highest branch, and dares to face the sun's low arch head-on and sing his heart out until his red breast feathers stand on end.

She knew that sound and she knew what she would see when she came to. First the dizzying lights in her eyes. Then she'd wait to figure out if she was still dreaming. Pieces of bark pressed into her cheek and a pinecone was wedged behind her ear. She opened her eyes. He was standing next to her. She expected he would be, but prone the way she was, unable yet to turn over, all she could see was one of his boots, glowing from the inside out, or so it appeared in this light. But he always glowed these days, didn't he? Now his other boot moved into her view as he shifted his weight; he'd been standing there a long time. If she could only pop up right now and surprise him, maybe she'd finally see him face-to-face, in actual time, her time, present-and-accounted-for time. She doubted it, though. He would stay until she recovered, she knew that. He always did. He'd stay until she recovered then disappear before she had a chance to tell him she had known about him for a long time.

Her blackouts were less frequent than they used to be and they were still unforeseen. It could happen anytime, though mostly it happened when she was alone. The only warning she got was a thirty-second window where the world appeared to thin out like a balloon stretched too far. Voices faded and her ears began to ring. At least, if she paid attention, it gave her a few moments to sit down, which she had done this time, on a stump next to the mountain path she was hiking on. She must have tipped over sometime after that.

A few minutes passed and she pulled herself up and brushed herself off. He was gone, of course. He lived on the edge of her trances and sometimes he'd visit her dreams. He'd been watching over her like this for more than two years, whenever the spells began to overcome her. The doctors guessed it was a carryover from the concussion. She might outgrow them, they said; then again, she might not.

She had named him Gabriel because at first she was convinced he was an angel. But after a while she thought differently. Now she believed he was a regular person with a gift, or curse, like her own, and that somehow he knew when she was in trouble and he'd seek her out. She didn't know why she thought that; maybe he told her in a dream. And she didn't know how he always found her. The details were still fuzzy but one thing rang true every time she encountered him: he was in love with her. She could feel it. And she might even be in love with him if the whole thing wasn't so weird.

Amanda sat back on the stump and dug a canteen out of her backpack. She took a long drink, closed her eyes, and let the cold water mend her parched throat. She poured a little over her head and let it drip down her face. What time was it? She fished for her watch. Four-thirty already? She had lost an hour. She felt lucky; often it was longer. She looked up at the sky.

It had been more than two years since she moved to the farm and, after a rough patch in the beginning, it was going pretty well. Mary Lynn, from the Silver Goose diner, had taken her under her wing, which Amanda was told was an extraordinary thing because Mary Lynn was particular about her associations, especially if you were from out-of-town. But Amanda guessed that she was doing it for Bernie's sake, and she was pretty sure Bernie had even prepped her for Amanda's impending arrival. So Amanda's assimilation wasn't as rough as it might have been. After all, she had Mary Lynn's good graces working for her as well as Bernie's legacy, and most people figured a young girl from a college town up north could be redeemed anyway, if she was given enough time.

One of Mary Lynn's particularly irritating crusades was her relentless pursuit to find Amanda a suitable boyfriend. Amanda was almost twenty, and over the course of two years Mary Lynn had fixed her up with a number of blind dates. She also attempted to corral her into more than a few church socials, which Amanda refused, although she thought it was amusing since Mary Lynn had herself given up on church-going a long time ago.

But to pacify Mary Lynn, Amanda figured she'd go along with the blind dates, which was the lesser of two evils. She felt awkward most of the time and it didn't help to be locked into Mary Lynn's well-established rules about courtship, one of which specified that a young lady should never entertain a gentleman in her home un-chaperoned. So they would rendezvous at the diner where Mary Lynn would serve them dinner before they left for the movies or the ballgame across town.

It all seemed very old fashioned and a little surreal but overall she enjoyed herself more than she expected. These boys were ground-ed and different then those back home and they definitely had better stories to tell. Take Morgan Greer, for instance, who lived at the farm next to hers. After Amanda spent half the evening drawing him out of his clam-like shyness, she eventually got him talking about the farm. But once he got going, he told her all kinds of things: about the steer he slaughtered in the fall, about how last spring he'd lost all his hair in a fire that started in the hayloft and nearly burnt the whole barn down. How a weaning calf got loose and climbed halfway up South Mountain looking for her mama then fell down an abandoned mineshaft before they could get to her. His father and brother had to lower Morgan into the shaft and he had to wrestle with her down there to keep her from falling further in. It was almost morning before he got the sling around her so they could hoist her back out. That was the day, he told Amanda, that he declared he'd never work for Winston Coal & Fuel. Not ever.

Morgan was the only one to ask her out twice, which didn't surprise her. She wasn't exactly a prize, after all. But instead of a date, she asked him if he would show her how to get the tractor running. Spring had moved in at the farm and was now a force to be reckoned with. The tractor, she discovered, was among her best allies. That and the goats she got from the Witherspoons down the road. Morgan was a natural teacher and was never condescending when illuminating the finer points of rear ballasts and PTOs. He even seemed genuinely impressed with what Bernie had taught her about the importance of lubrication. She learned quickly, driven by her promise to Bernie to keep the farm going.

Morgan came by fairly regularly after that to help her when the bales needed to be put up or the fences needed repair. Mary Lynn said it was obvious that Morgan had other intentions, that he was curious about more than the farm. When Amanda brushed her off, she told Amanda that she was too picky, that Morgan was a fine young man from a good family. "You've got to learn, Amanda," she said, "that the men around here will not throw themselves at you. They've got too much pride. They may do things different where you come from, but here, a man needs a little encouragement from a woman."

Now she had crossed the line. Amanda stood her ground, faced Mary Lynn head on, and told her off right then and there, making it perfectly clear that she did not need nor want a boyfriend, nor a husband for that matter, that being alone suited her just fine. In fact (she was shouting now) she had every intention of running the farm by herself, the way Bernie did. She expected Mary Lynn to fight back and she was ready for it, but instead, Mary Lynn smiled at Amanda like she was one of her own.

Amanda laughed out loud at the memory of it. She got up, stretched her legs, and looked down the path. She had a few hours of daylight left, still enough time to make it to Chalahume Falls. She picked up her pack and started walking. It didn't take long for the rhythm of her footsteps to clear her head, and the prospect of revisiting that magical place excited her. It was, after all, the place where she was transformed. Where her dreaming gained weight and brightness and meaning. It was where the terrors and hollowness were put to rest. It was where she was reborn.

Now as she approached the falls, its effervescence landed on her skin. It happened two years ago to the day, she remembered well. It was an event even she never expected: a meeting of her two worlds in real time. A battle of great proportion, a combat among titans and she in the middle. Her very soul was at war that day, and she survived it.

How to explain her otherworld at that fragile moment? The world that had emerged after the bike accident from the unchartered depths of her dreaming, where leaks in her unconsciousness were no longer shored by the natural protection of healthy neurons, gateways now blown apart and open to invasion. This is how her dreaming had evolved. Over the first months at the farm, she had slowly become vulnerable to these rank presences pressing upon her unlicensed awareness. She felt and knew too much about this empty world where the principles of void and chaos trumped everything else, where what existed there was powerful in its unsubstantial and lifeless persistence. And it was growing.

By the time she found the falls that day, she was desperate and isolated beyond comprehension. Her only thread to hope was Gabriel, whom she would see in her dreams now and then in that same way she did the first time, when she watched him move through the Mighty Mart and could feel what he was feeling, knowing he had visions the same way she did, especially in times of stress, when the pressure of real time gained strength squeezing the otherworld into the forefront where it would take over. She'd see him clearest at those times, not as a participant but as a bystander. A witness to his agony. It always made her cry: she'd cry for his suffering and she'd cry because she believed he was the one person in the universe who shared her own experience.

She had set out that morning two years ago to end this madness. To once and for all make peace with it. It had worn her out, the undertow of the otherworld now consuming even her waking hours. The visions, the dreams, Gabriel. She was a fool for entertaining the possibility that any of it could be true. True or not, there was no denying that it overcame her. Her closest friends knew about the spells, knew they were worsening. Mary Lynn especially was keeping a close eye not knowing exactly what to do but making damn sure her charge didn't slip away altogether. But Amanda hadn't told anyone about *him*, not Mary Lynn, not Dehlia, and she began to suspect that she hadn't because deep down her muse was whispering, "Gabriel is an illusion, Amanda, a trick of a bruised brain."

That's when she decided to give up. What if she *was* only pretending he was real, imagining things that weren't true. It was time, she decided, to get on with her life or end it. She needed something more to hang on to than a ghost. She'd heard about the falls only a few miles down this path. She'd go there and settle matters for good. If there was anything to any of this, she'd find it at the river. If she didn't, then she'd bury it there.

She had climbed out to the middle of the river on the back of a smooth flat boulder wet with spray. The falling water hammered away on the bank opposite and she watched the current spin into a confusion of foaming eddies below her. A train rumbled in the distance and she listened as it approached. Louder and louder it sounded as it clattered over the rails and echoed off the irregular angles rising from the rocky gap. The whistle blew and she jumped. Suddenly the engine and its freight appeared screaming over the tracks, roaring through the notch a hundred feet above her, the hounds of hell shrieking around the turn that led to the old trestle.

The sound was unbearable and she nearly fell. She pressed her hands to her ears and her world began to thin out. She moved to the center of the boulder and lay down.

Instantly the otherworld took over and she found herself standing on the old trestle that crossed the fault where the mountain opened to a chasm. In the distance she saw the Chalahume plummet over a towering precipice, its frothing sheets breaking into riverlets as it tumbled over the cliff's stony outcroppings. At the bottom of the cliff a large granite shelf jutted out creating a platform where water collected into a protected pool before continuing its journey under the trestle and downstream toward Porterstown.

It was nighttime in the dream and looking out from the bridge toward the cliff, she saw the silhouettes of two men standing in the river. All about them the water was in turmoil, churning and bucking over and around the formation of stone that protected them from the current. Although they were in shadow, backlit by the moon, she knew it was Gabriel because she could feel him. As she studied them from her perch on the bridge, she saw them bow their heads. Then all at once the man grabbed Gabriel by the shoulders and pushed him under the water. As he sank, it was as if she went under too. Suddenly the night went quiet, and the thunder of the water ceased. The quiet grew and grew and soon the rushing falls slowed until they stopped altogether. All around her the water stilled until the whole river was a sheet of glass. She was lifted out of time and place into a realm of silent fascination, not ecstasy exactly, but an awareness of an all-consuming understanding, as if peace was a living thing and she was dwelling there. The water, the stillness, the enveloping elation, the dream that was not a dream. She recognized it as something she had always known, but only just now remembered. Like waking from a long slumber at the sound of her mother's voice. Her soul swelled with life and hope and relief. It was finished.

Now, still in her otherworld, she saw Gabriel submerged in the dark pool, then slowly the water began to stir. Through its silent and radiant surface, she watched him rise up, beads of light falling from his hair. He looked up and saw her standing on the trestle. The pull of his gaze across the distant bank set her on fire. The man prayed over him and still he stared. "Amen," said the man. "Amen," said Amanda.

She woke up to the same attentive moon she had seen in the dream. Lucent clouds netted the golden sphere and filtered its wide beam upon the pool below her exciting the mist that had gathered there. Amanda looked up and greeted that bright and happy orb. She opened her hand and let its radiance fall on her palm. It was her time now. Amidst eternity that coursed through the ages, under the comfort and protection of her lunar sentinel, she knew this moment was her moment, it was her time. Quickly and silently, she undressed. Then she stood with her toes pressed on the rock's cool rough edge and gazed at her reflection quaking on the water. She filled her lungs with the night's sweet fragrance and dove in.

That was two years ago. It was the day the nightmares ceased. Her visions continued but rather than overcome her with confusion and fear, they informed her now. They had thrown her a line to sanity, a world beyond her invaders, a supreme wisdom more reasoned and kind than anything she had ever known. Over time, the dread that had relentlessly haunted her diminished. And now two years out, she could scarcely remember the extent to which that dark oppression had terrorized her.

"And that may well be the kindest gift of all," she mused while standing on the riverbank. To have marked in time and place the death of her captor, slain there on that cool spring day two years ago in the still small pool before her. One by one she tossed the blooms she had gathered along the path. Late May roses with their lingering sweetness, the saffron heads of tiger lilies, the crepe clusters of redbud blossoms, each landing gently on the clear water, their petals drawing shimmering trails as they floated gently downstream and out of sight.

The river was beautiful and she never tired of looking at it. But lately a thought kept nagging at her. The river was changing. How was that possible? She didn't know, yet she could see it. With the memory of her baptism fresh in her mind, she looked up at the falls. No longer did they batter and beat the cliff with a terrible fervor. The torrent had slowed down remarkably and its banks had grown wide through the receding water.

Maybe it was true, though. Maybe it was changing. Just yesterday at the diner, she had overheard the railroad men talking of such things. Mary Lynn had joined in, ranting and shaking her head over something that was happening at the reservoir upstream. She'd have to ask her about it.

Her thoughts were interrupted by the shrill sound of a whistle echoing through the gorge. It blew again. Two shorts and a long. It was Eugene Gilbert's signature call, all is well in Porterstown, he was announcing as he approached the trestle on his way to the end of the line at the Winston stop.

The track ran close to the cliff's edge circumventing the river over a natural formation of granite that crossed a hundred feet overhead. She waited for the engine to appear. Finally here she came: The old No. 49, a proud steam locomotive destined for obscurity but for the tenacious passion of these railroad men. Amanda could feel the ground shake at the engine's advance. She broke off a long branch to flag Mr. Gilbert as he lumbered past. He spotted her down below and puffed two short and fluty whistles in friendly acknowledgment before the caboose disappeared around the oxbow bend that led past her farm to the mines beyond.

19

"We'll set up here," Joe said, pointing to a map he had stretched across the table in the empty dining car.

"I don't know, Rev," Danny responded, "that's mighty close to the Winston Coal & Fuel entrance where ever one of their thugs is likely to be waitin'. We'd do better to set up down here," he said tapping the map.

"We could, Danny," Joe said, "but it's got to be done in the bright light of day out in the open. Remember, we've got a camera crew coming down to document the whole thing and they'll need plenty of room. The field above the ridge outside WCF's west entrance is broad and without trees or other obstacles. We've got the best view of the impoundment from there and the refuse coal they're dumping. That's the only piece left to document, and we may only get this one chance. Plus technically it's on the back parcel of Mrs. Mahoney's farm so they can't get us for trespassing. Let their cronies stand around all day if they want. They're not going to cause trouble if the WCF knows there's a chance they'll find themselves on the evening news."

Cody opened the door to the passenger car. "Bill sent me to tell you we're about twelve miles outside Herston."

"I declare, look who's here. You think you're some kind of wizard or somethin', appearing out of thin air and all. How the hell are you?" Danny said, clapping Cody's hand in a firm shake.

"I'm doin' just fine. I jumped a ride at Copper Gorge. Glad to see you've not changed a bit over these last two years, Danny. Still lookin' like somethin' the cat drug in." Danny roared and Cody turned to Joe. "How you been, Rev?"

Joe's broad and affectionate smile was a welcome greeting. "Thank the good Lord you've arrived, Jeremiah. One more interrogation from Martha about your whereabouts would have done me in for good. And I'm warning you, she has not forgotten that you up and left without telling her goodbye, and then traveling all about the country as the spirit moves with no word back at all. 'Even a child can pick up a phone,' she said just this morning. You are on dangerous ground, young man, and I'll not be standing between you and Martha on that sorry day of reckoning."

Cody laughed, "Thanks, Rev, happy to see you too."

They rolled into the Herston yard, where Eugene Gilbert eased the No. 49 into the crossover switch where her cars were humped down the slope to be loaded for the trip back.

Bill Jenkins popped open the cab door. "Come on, Eugene. You ready to eat?"

"You go ahead," Eugene said to Walter, his fireman, "I'll join you after awhile. I want to check in with the back shop to make sure they tend to her running gear properly."

"Nothin' too good for our sweet No. 49," Bill said. "Suit yourself." The holster came aboard and they detrained so Eugene could roll her into the roundhouse.

It was the brainchild of Bill and Eugene and it had taken them more than a decade to pull it off. The No. 49 steam engine on the Brinklow line was the last of her kind to ride through those Blue Ridge mountain towns on the western side of Virginia, east Tennessee, and into the coal country of West Virginia. She was a mixed train in her day, carrying both passengers and freight down the two-hundred-and-fifty mile line from Winston in the north to Herston in the south.

More than a decade before, in the 1950s, when the railroad industry was converting to the more powerful and efficient diesels,

Winston Coal & Fuel sold the Brinklow line. "Those big wigs in New York made hundreds of millions on the sale and that's no joke," Bill told Cody, "and they promised all of us that the profits would go toward helpin' the miners by improving safety and securing jobs. They stood up right there at the union meeting and had the gall to let go that bald faced lie. Ain't that right Walter?"

Walter nodded. "Yes indeed. Got two brothers that was there. And they haven't seen no pay increase in years. The only thing they say increased is the work."

Bill told Cody that when the Brinklow line changed hands, its steam engines were put out to pasture, some of them literally. It took more than a little artful cajoling by Bill and Eugene to get the good people of the Winston Town Council to agree to appropriate the No. 49 before she was scrapped, and she eventually found refuge in the abandoned roundhouse outside town not far from Bill's place. Ten years later and with help from the local historical societies and other philanthropists, the No. 49 hit the rails once again. This time, pulling a tender, two tourist cars, five boxcars, and a red caboose, she transported nostalgic sightseers as well as the eclectic wares of the small businesses that had long ago established along the line.

Bill, Walter, and Cody joined Joe and Danny at Herston's Tri-State truck stop situated between the northbound track and interstate 81.

"Will it be the usual for you boys?" Betty asked, pencil to pad. Sam and Betty Churnak were longtime friends of Bill and Walter going all the way back to their early days of railroading. "Nice to see you again, Reverend," she said to Joe. "You let me know if the rubberneckin' bothers you and I'll remind our regulars about their manners. Eatin' here is a privilege and they can take their appetite elsewhere if they feel less than blessed by the presence of a man of the cloth such as yourself."

"It's okay, Betty," Joe said, "I'm kind of used to it but I appreciate the gesture."

"Well I do not believe you would be appreciatin' the gesture I just observed at booth three, but then he's a newcomer, probably hitched a ride with T.J. Excuse me while I have a little chat with our newest patron."

"Winnin' hearts and minds all the way up and down the ridge since I've been gone, eh Joe?" Cody observed.

"Yes and no. The community is becoming more polarized, no doubt about it. Not about race, though—about WCF. Union negotiations broke down again, this time around the issue of the new impoundment. The company finally made small concessions regarding wages and benefits, but they've done nothing to improve the refuse and sludge that's piling up on Pond 3. To date they've not complied with state engineering standards issued last fall and as far as we know they still have no plans for building an emergency spillway and overflow system. The arbitrator's engineers are telling us that without a way to handle excessive runoff a washout is inevitable."

Betty returned to the table and passed around their steamy plates of chip beef on biscuits and mustard greens.

"What are you goin' to do?" Cody asked draining the last of his sweet tea.

"We're going public. That's why I asked you to come back."

"Wait a minute," Danny interjected, "I thought he was AWOL, that no one knew where he was."

Cody shrugged and Joe added, "That's mostly true, but Jeremiah and I made an agreement before he left. He'd check in now and then and I'd keep quiet about it."

"Why all the secrecy, Jeremiah?" Danny asked. "You got somethin' to hide?"

"Maybe, at least I like to let on that I do. Mostly I wanted some room, some time alone. Had some things to sort out."

"It's been almost two years. That's a helluva lot of sortin'. What've you been doin'?"

"Playin', in New York mostly, but travelin' some too. There's a great music scene happenin' on the other side of these mountains."

"You playin' country?"

"Some, a little of everything, really. Ended up on the road for a while with a country band. But there's a lot of mixin' it up going on. Blues with country, country with rock 'n roll. Good time for hearin' and playin' all kinds of music."

"And you didn't invite me to tag along. Man, that's cruel."

"Guess it is, but like I say, I'm kind of a loner and the roaming suits me. Maybe the army does that to you, I don't know. So I was in Texas a few month ago, Dallas I think, and I met up with some pretty big names. Just the right place at the right time, I guess. They were in the middle of their tour and needed some backup guitar and piano. The pay was pretty good so I signed on. The tour finished in New York and the band's really startin' to take off. They've already booked dates at a couple of stadiums and festivals."

"Get outta here. Anyone we've I heard of?" Danny asked.

"I don't know, it doesn't matter, does it? I decided to quit anyway."

"You got to be kiddin' me. You just started making a name for yourself outside these hills and you quit. Man, you are crazy."

"That's a well established fact," Cody laughed.

"Why did you quit?" Joe asked.

"I got good advice. One night after that last gig in New York, I was pretty keyed up so I went to an all-night club where I was hangin' out at a lot, where the music was good and the stage was open to anyone who could really play. I sat at the bar for awhile until other musicians began to show up to see if anything was happenin', just like I was. Must've been a full moon or something because it was a night they came in droves. A couple of them were well known, and not just in the city. A buddy of mine, a conga player, showed. I helped carry his drums in and when he was settin' up, he asked if I'd sit in.

"We played for a couple of hours, just jammin' and foolin' around," Cody continued, chewing on the ice in his glass. "We all did some songs we'd each worked up. It was great, really great. And when things started to break up, my eye turned to a man sitting at a table in a dim corner of the bar and he flagged me over. 'Let me buy you a drink,' he said. I said, 'Sure,' and sat down. It was right about then that I recognized who he was, and I realized I was about to have a beer with a guy more famous than the pope. So we sat there awhile not sayin' much watching the stage and listening. When the set ended he ordered another round and then said he'd seen me play at Carnegie Hall earlier that night."

"You played at Carnegie Hall?" Danny moaned. "Now you've gone too far."

"That's what I thought, but it gets better. He said he liked what

I was doin', said my songs had feelin'. I might be headin' somewhere
big if I wanted it bad enough, and kept workin' hard at it the way I
was. I couldn't believe it, coming from him. We were quiet a long
spell after that and then he asked me what I intended to do with my
life. I said I didn't know, play music, I guess, had another tour comin'
up. He said that I reminded him of himself a few years back, called
to perform like a moth to flame. Exciting and irresistible, is how he
put it. But then he said I should be careful, that I should think long
and hard before I decide. I asked him why. He said, 'because if you
continue down this road, which appears to be your intention, fame
just might come knockin'. Fame is a hard mistress,' he said, 'and she'll
make you a prisoner in your own skin.' Then he got up from the table,
shook my hand, and left by the backdoor." Cody leaned back in his
chair.

"You're shittin' me," was Danny's reply. "Who was it?"

"I can't say."

"Why not?"

"'Cause he asked me not to. He said if I told the story he'd be
indebted to me if I'd keep his name out of it. So I've told the story
and honored his wishes too."

"I don't buy, it," Walter chimed in chewing on his food. "You're
spinnin' another one of your tales just to make yourself look good or
to save face from havin' to crawl back here with nothing to show for
it. It's one or the other."

"Maybe I am. Can't fault a guy for tryin', but I quit just the
same, so it doesn't really matter if it's true or not. When Joe asked me
to come back, I'd already decided, so it was nice to have somewhere
to go."

"Blue Jay, this is Devil Dog," crackled a voice on Bill's radio,
"Do you copy?"

"This is Blue Jay, you 'bout done down there? Over."

"She's ready to go. Will you get Betty to send a poke? Looks
like I'll be eatin' on the ride back. Over."

"She's way ahead of you. Got your supper right here. We're on
our way. Blue Jay, Out."

Night was falling early on the cloudy hills as they made their
way across the parking lot to the yard. Cody lit up and inhaled the

blue smoke.

"Still craving tobacco, I see, but lost your appetite for fame, eh, Jeremiah?" Joe asked.

"I suppose. Give me fortune any day, but you can keep fame. I saw what it had done to that man and I knew that even a small portion coming my way would cost me more freedom than I can spare. That's no kinda life for me and that's all there is to it." Up ahead Walter was already climbing into the cab to help the holster finish feeding wood into the engine's firebox.

"So what kinda scheme you got cooked up, Joe?" Cody asked.

"Music," he smiled. "Don't worry though. This venue sure won't make you famous, I'm certain of that. And you can bet you won't find your fortune there either."

"Let me be the judge of that."

20

Amanda was surprised at the turnout. For some time, Mary Lynn had bothered her about reviving the Yellow Bird jubilees and she had been reluctant.

"Times are gettin' hard for a lot of folks and they need reasons to get together," she told her. "Your grandmother knew that back two generations ago when she started the potluck suppers. That was right after your granddaddy was killed. There was many of us who had lost our men on that day and it was a way for us to help each other. Some of us, including Bernie, was in a family way so we knew we had to band together to get through it. It began with just us women and the babies, but then the men started comin' too 'cause the food was so good, and later for Ernie's beer. Then of course the music started and then the dancin' so we decided to call it the jubilee. After awhile, the babies grew up and most kept comin' and then before you knew it, they was bringin' their own children. She kept the suppers goin' all those years, until she got sick, of course. After that there was no one who was willin' to pick it up. Wouldn't be the same if it weren't done at the Yellow Bird, they said. People miss it, they miss her. You'd be doing good by her to start again."

She looked into Amanda's face which had nearly turned to stone by this time. "Aw, come on now, it ain't that bad, and I'll help you. I'll tell you what, let's have a little look out back on the patio and I'll show you how it was done." Amanda surrendered as she followed her out the door. And so the preparations began.

The jubilee commenced on a warm and breezy Saturday evening on the first day of summer and Amanda sat on the patio wall watching the crowd at the table. The festivities were soon underway as if there had been no lapse at all, or so it seemed. People brought the same dishes they always had, Ernie filled the same barrels with ice and bottles of beer and soda. Everyone sat in their usual places at the big table and told all the familiar stories. The young people sat in chairs along the wall or on the patio floor balancing plates heaped with lasagna, macaroni and cheese, Jello salad, and bread pudding. The same old ladies fell into habits of refilling coffee and cutting pie and the old men took turns clearing away the dishes. It made Amanda happy to see her grandmother through their eyes and before the night was out, nearly every one of them made an effort to share some stories about her.

"Did your granny ever tell you about how she fell in love?" asked Mrs. Cunningham, with mischief in her eye. Amanda hadn't really thought about Bernie as a lover and she wasn't sure if she wanted to think about it now. But Mrs. Cunningham looked like she was the oldest person there, and in the way of old people, she lit right into her story before Amanda had a chance to stop her.

"I am your granddaddy's first cousin," she began in her soft-spoken manner, "and I am here to tell you, Matthew Elias Abernathy was the handsomest man ever born to this side of South Mountain. It is also my contention that he was amongst the finest individuals to ever set foot in all of Prescott County. People here still think of him as a war hero, did you know that? No I guess not. Bernie would not have talked much about it. You see, sometimes even the passing of years is not enough to mend a heart gone silent with loss."

She proceeded to tell Amanda of the letters he sent home to his sister while he was stationed in France during the Great War, letters that came to Mrs. Cunningham after his sister passed. "I brought this tonight to give to you," Mrs. Cunningham said. She unfastened the large clasp on her sizable pocketbook and carefully withdrew a small square of brown leather. She handed it to Amanda. "Open it, dear," she said.

The leather was smooth except where the hands of her relatives had worn it through to the cardboard underneath. She opened it and there in the gilt-cut oval smiled her grandfather. It made Amanda smile too. He was handsome, just as she claimed, and so young. His pose was not stiff like she'd seen in other old war photos, sepia soldiers standing stick-straight, riffles at their sides, and staring blankly at points unknown. No, her grandfather was sitting at a sidewalk café, in Paris, she imagined, drinking wine and laughing at the camera as if he hadn't a care in the world. On the soft suede opposite he had inscribed, "Dearest Esther, I am the happiest man on earth. It took a war and an ocean for me to meet my bride. We leave for home tomorrow. Your favorite doughboy, Matty."

"He was a gem, that one," Mrs. Cunningham continued. "He was stationed in Marne during the second battle, with the First Battalion Tenth Engineers of the American Expeditionary Forces. He shipped out just before all hell broke loose, and it *was* hell over there, too." She paused a long time, staring over Amanda's head, gathering her recollections.

She tapped her chin. "I remember that by the time his first letter arrived, he had already been injured – some shrapnel to the shoulder, he said, and he ended up in a hospital in a place called Dax. It was the hospital (if you could call it that, glorified tent is what it was) where your grandmother was stationed. Shortly thereafter, the rest of his company was pummeled with the German mustard gas, and they arrived in Dax blinded or unable to breathe. As fate would have it, a few days prior, the lieutenant nurse was dispatched to another camp, leaving Bernie to tend to the patients by herself. She was only about twenty then but when she was put in charge, Matty said she took to it like nobody's business. At that time Matty was still too injured to go back to the front but he was well enough to move around some if he kept his arm tight in the sling. Because he was the only soldier not entirely bedridden, Bernie pressed him into service as her second in command. Oh how he loved to tell it. She was an unstoppable force, a tyrant of a boss, he'd say, workin' them night and day, lookin' after those boys and their terrible wounds and broken hearts, and they were boys, nearly all of them." She went silent for a time and then stood for no apparent reason.

"Is something wrong, Mrs. Cunningham?" Amanda asked, standing too. She stared at Amanda oddly, like she had forgotten what she was going to say, or maybe where she was. It took a few minutes for her to regain her composure.

"Law no, honey, nothing except an eighty-year-old body which protests more than you can imagine. My bones get all stiff and sore if I sit too long. There now, that's better," she said, smoothing the creases that persisted on the front of her dress. "Oh there's Teddy pacin' like a caged lion. Looks like he's ready to go. I tell you what," she squeezed Amanda's hand. "Matthew'd be real proud to see how you've kept the place goin'. I can't tell you how much I've enjoyed the jubilee. I said just the other day at my prayer time, 'Dear God Almighty, sweet Jesus, just let me live to see another jubilee on South Mountain.' And darn if he didn't give it to me." Mrs. Cunningham draped the vinyl strap of her pocketbook over her arm and tottered across the patio to join her son.

On the other side of the gathering on the bookstore's grassy yard, two Adirondack chairs were perched on a rise overlooking the receding landscape. She and Dehlia had dragged them out there when they were exploring the Yellow Bird for the first time. The view was a comfort to Amanda. From there she could see the fields and paddocks, the farmhouse sitting on the shady corner where the roads intersected. She could see the farm's mossy lane wind between the farmhouse and the barn where it followed the road up the hill to the bookstore. And she could see past the house to the driveway that pitched downward around the barn to its first floor at the bottom of the hill. Beyond that, at the edge of her property, she could see the stand of pines and black walnut that stretched northward, where further out, the Chalahume, and the rail that ran along the cliff above it, passed southwest to the trestle at Twin Gap and then on towards Porterstown.

Amanda walked across the damp yard and sat in the empty chair next to Eppy. "Hungry?" she asked.

"You kiddin', another bite and I might explode." The redhead rubbed her swollen belly which all but enveloped her lap.

"Are you okay?"

"As okay as a bloated cow can be."

Eppy was Mary Lynn's granddaughter. She had left home and moved in with Mary Lynn six months ago when she discovered she was pregnant. Mary Lynn had counted on Amanda to befriend her, "Lord knows, she ain't going to have it easy," she told Amanda. While she hated these mandates from Mary Lynn, it turned out that she and Eppy hit it off.

Eppy was not yet eighteen when she was unofficially disowned by her parents in Glen Mills. "It's their loss," she said to Amanda when they met. "They didn't count on me holdin' my ground. They were hell-bent on marryin' me off and I wouldn't hear of it. That's why I wouldn't tell them who the father was. They were changed people after that, concerned more about their standin' in the community than about me. That's when I called Mamaw." Eppy still had the face and freckles of a cherub, but now, months later, as she sat watching the sun creep slowly toward the ridge, her gaze was hard and her mouth was set in a tight line against all that was to come.

"Do you ever wish you had married him?" Amanda asked her.

She thought a minute, then said, "No, I guess not. When I think about raisin' this baby alone, I sometimes wish I had a husband to help me. It scares me sometimes, bein' alone. But no, I didn't love him. It was one night of what was hardly what I'd call passion. Let's just say, he did not exactly meet my expectations."

"Well you have Mary Lynn on your side, that's some consolation."

"The consolation prize, you mean," she laughed.

"Speaking of romance," Amanda ventured, "Mrs. Cunningham told me something about a wild love affair between Bernie and my grandfather. Do you know anything about it?"

"Matthew's war bride? That's what some people on his side still call Bernie," she said sipping a coke. "Matthew Elias Abernathy, the war hero. I heard Mrs. Cunningham first tell it when I was little when I'd be visitin' Mamaw and we'd have lunch with her at the diner. I've heard it a hundred times since then too. She hasn't told it lately though. Mamaw says she's touched with the dementia. But it was romantic, I even thought so as a kid.

"She said that during the war in France, Bernie became the

head nurse in a barracks they had turned into a hospital; it was a big job for a lady, especially in those days and for one as young as your grandmother. Your granddaddy was there recovering from a bad shoulder wound they say he got by savin' another man's life. Things got worse at the hospital and soon all the beds was full of dyin' men and only Bernie there to look after them. They say Matthew was smitten, a case of love at first sight, and he vowed to marry her or die tryin'.

"It was Christmas eve and all the men had been bathed, the fresh bandages had been applied, and extra doses of laudanum rendered, which was a Christmas gift from Bernie to help them sleep through the night. Before she went back to her hut for a few hours sleep, she gathered her instruments and equipment and opened the door to the storeroom. There at a candlelit table sat Matthew. He had planned everything. The little Christmas tree in the corner covered in tinsel, a roasted bird, a loaf of bread, a bottle of wine on the table, unheard of luxuries in wartime. He reached behind him and the music began to play on a scratchy Victrola. Without a word, he took her by the hand and they danced slow and long across the storeroom floor." Eppy swayed slowly back and forth. "Finally he led her to the shinin' tree where a single gift hung from a thin bow. A silver ring. He placed it on her finger and smiled when she saw he had hung mistletoe in the rafter above. It was their first kiss, he said. 'The kiss heard round the world.'"

The final rays of the dimming day withdrew behind the trees when Amanda heard the low mournful pull of a bow on strings. "There you are," said Mary Lynn out of breath from her fast approach. "We've been lookin' for you two. We're ready to start. Eppy, you up to playin' some?"

"Yeah, but I won't be fittin' no dulcimer across this lap, that's for sure." She turned to Amanda. "You got a table I might use?" Amanda helped haul her out of the deep construction of the Adirondack chair and they walked back to the bookstore.

Firelight from the patio's large stone grill danced on the cello Doris Canton balanced against a swag of skirt that hung between her straddled legs. Beside her, Mr. Greer, Morgan's father, was tuning his banjo, and Morgan and his uncle were picking out harmonies on their guitars. Eppy sidled to the card table where her mountain dulcimer awaited and she began to strum. Her face grew quiet and relaxed, her eyes closed, and her brows bent slightly in concentration. Amanda could see that Eppy was as familiar with her instrument as she was with her own breathing. It was a beautiful sound, like the ringing of bells, soft echoes from distant hills, all but forgotten ties to the old myths and magic. If memory were music, Amanda thought, it would sound like this.

She popped the top on a cold beer and handed it to the man who was maneuvering his wheelchair closer to the band. "How 'bout another one, Mr. Lawson?"

"That's mighty nice of you, Amanda. Don't mind if I do." She opened one for herself and sat down next to him. "Sounds really nice," she said.

He nodded and took a swig. "There's no one on this good earth who brews anything better than this. How's Eppy gettin' on?"

"Doctor says another two weeks before the baby comes. She's doing pretty well, considering."

"Well we may not be known for much in this little holler, but we are a people that knows how to look after one another."

"We are that, for sure," Amanda acknowledged. "Mr. Lawson? Eppy mentioned that you and my mom went to grade school together. Is that right?"

"Yes indeed. I even had a little crush on her," he chuckled. "I remember calling her my wild Iris rose and I chased her all around the school yard. I was heartbroken when she left."

"Was that when Bernie sent her to New Jersey to live with her sister?"

"That's right. Times got really tough for Bernie. Hell, it was tough on ever'one here back then. But Bernie was havin' a particularly hard time of it, bein' a widow and all. Her tenants had moved out of the farmhouse and she wasn't getting' much in the way of income from the bookstore. She was afraid of what might happen to Iris if things got any worse. So she arranged to have her live with her sister outside Newark in New Jersey, is what my mama told me. For just a little while, she said, at least until Bernie got back on her feet." Mr. Lawson pressed the bottle to his forehead. "Now that feels good. We could use a little breeze through the gorge just about now. So anyway, a month turned into a year, a year into two, and soon Iris had a new set of friends and had gotten right close to her auntie. Bernie would go up to visit when she could but after a while, especially once she was in high school, Iris simply didn't want to come back home. It weren't easy on Bernie, lettin' her baby go like that. But her sister was good to Iris and was happy to have her stay on. So Bernie allowed it, believing Iris would get a better upbringin'."

"Do you think she did?" Amanda asked. "Get a better upbringing, I mean?"

"I don't know. I think deep down each of us believes our own people have cornered the market on upbringin', especially when they have happy memories of their own childhoods. That was why Bernie dearly loved those summers you came to stay with her. It may not have meant much to you, being just a child and all, but it meant the world to Bernie."

A bright moon rose overhead and soon the people were dancing and wheeling to spirited renditions of Black Mountain Rag, Cornbread, and the other old favorites from years ago.

21

"Frankenstein?"

"Hey, preacher, it's your book not mine," Cody reminded him. He slipped the book back onto the shelf and pulled out the thin volume next to it, *The Articles of Confederation of Perpetual Union*.

"Martha's ready to serve dinner. Want to join us?"

"When are you Yankees going to understand that it's called supper? Dinner was hours ago. Don't get me wrong, though. I'm not one to look a gift horse in the mouth," and he jumped up and followed Joe up the stairs.

As they sat down at the table, Cody could hear Martha in the kitchen. "You've been real charitable toward me, Rev," Cody said, "lettin' me stay in your basement while I'm in town, and all. I hope one day I can return the favor."

"I may be cashing in a few favors before you know it. Tomorrow's not likely to be a cakewalk. It could turn ugly pretty quick, in which case I'll need your help in any number of ways."

Cody knew what he meant. The First Annual Roundhouse Revival could go off without a hitch, with the town's good citizens enjoying the festivities and the day's public service and safety seminars. Or Winston Coal & Fuel could ensure that no revival so close to their operation would happen again for a long time to come.

Martha brought out a basket of homemade rolls and a bowl heaped with steaming mashed potatoes. "Why don't you boys start passing these around while I get everything else served up. Wouldn't want it to get cold." From the kitchen, she handed Joe a platter of meatloaf, some lima beans, gravy, and beverages. "That should do it," she said as she sat down.

Joe gave the blessing and then served himself a generous slice of meatloaf. "No scrimping tonight. Tomorrow's going to be a long day. Jeremiah, I could use a little of that gravy over here," he said stretching out a hand. "Martha, are you going into town after dinner?"

"I've got to," Martha said. "Mrs. Mahoney will be disappointed otherwise. She wants to show me all the supplies stockpiled by the Porterstown ladies auxiliary. She says it'll take a couple of boxcars to haul it up to the Mahoney farm."

"Before Joe and I were married," Martha explained to Cody, "I worked at the Red Cross disaster relief center in New York, starting up first response and first aid training programs in the local boroughs. In fact, that's where I met Joe." She continued to explain to Cody that during the weekly pancake breakfasts at the Porterstown fire-house the previous fall, the drift of many a conversation continually turned to the Winston impoundment and the water dammed behind it. "As God is my witness," Mrs. Mahoney had said to Martha who sat across from her at the dining hall table, "just yesterday when I was callin' our cows up from the pasture, I noticed that the creek runnin' through there looked darker than is usual. So I scooped up a handful, and sure 'nough, there was coal sludge in the water. Now I ask you, Mrs. Price," she said pointing her fork at her, "have you ever thought about what would transpire if that dam should crack or slump? Ever one is talkin' about it yet not a single thing is gettin' done."

That's when Martha told her about her work planning the Red Cross fairs. They were fun events with food and music and games for children. But they also held seminars on emergency prepared-ness. "What made it work," Martha explained, "was the fact that the people in the neighborhoods organized it. They determined what would be useful and what kind of training made sense."

"Why Mrs. Price," Mrs. Mahoney said, "I do believe you are

on to somethin'. Yes indeed, I am sure of it. What we need is our own fair. I tell you what. We can do it on our farm. It's easy enough to get up there from Twin Gap and Porterstown. And I am certain my Samuel would agree (had he survived to see the opportunity, God love him). There's plenty of room on the pasture that runs along the ridge, and it's the parcel closest to the old roundhouse." She leaned into the table and spoke in confiding tones. "It's a perfect plan. We could do it on a Sunday, after church. That way we could talk Eugene Gilbert and Bill Jenkins into firing up the ol' 49 to bring people up from the valley. People who would not make the trip otherwise. I feel the call, Mrs. Price. I am God inspired," she said, a flush rising in her cheeks. "We will call it the Roundhouse Revival. Yes, that's what we'll do. We will get the people up here for training and they can see for themselves what the coal is doin' to the river." She craned her neck around. "Now where did you say your husband is seated?" She was already out of her chair and half way across the room before Martha could say a word.

In the months that followed Mrs. Mahoney had rallied every ladies club, sewing circle, and Wednesday night prayer meeting across both denominations in Winston, Twin Gap, Porterstown, and even south to Copper Gorge. She gained the support of the men at the Lions Club and Kiwanis Club all along the line, and she even managed to get on the agenda of the union's monthly meeting in Winston. And now nearly a year later, the Roundhouse Revival was ready to roll.

Martha groaned a little when she got up from the table to clear the dishes. "I don't mind admitting it, Joe, I am simply unable to keep up with Mrs. Mahoney, and she's old enough to be my mother. That woman is on a mission and is not to be deterred. She can rest easy now, though, and reap the good that she has sewn. As near as I can tell, you are likely to see record numbers tomorrow."

"I certainly hope so. I heard from one of the networks this afternoon. They say they're sending someone from the D.C. bureau. They're hoping for more than a human interest story."

After they cleared the table, Martha left to pick up Anna before heading to town.

"Let's go downstairs, Jeremiah," Joe said. "There's something I want to show you."

Cody sat on the basement's worn couch and Joe opened the desk drawer. "See what you make of this," Joe said, handing him an envelope. Cody lifted the flap and opened the note. It consisted of block letters cut and pasted at odd angles. He read it out load: *"Keep it up and you'll be the next Emmett Till."*

Cody handed it back. "I gotta have a smoke. You wanna come outside with me?" They stepped out the basement door to the concrete landing and Cody drew a pack of Camels out of his pocket. "Man, the game's been raised to a whole new level, Rev. When did you get it?"

"The day before yesterday. Guess we've hit a nerve."

"Does Martha know about it?"

"No."

Cody took a long draw. "Can't blame you for not tellin' her. Wouldn't do any good." He let his thoughts mingle with the smoke that he sent whirling skyward. "You've been livin' here long enough to know they ain't kiddin'."

"I know. Except that I checked it out. We think it came from New York."

They looked out into the silent starry night.

"Look," Joe continued. "If it is, in fact, from New York, then we can assume it's a ploy from the WCF execs to keep us from making the issues known. That's an easier situation for us to manipulate than the rave rantings of a lone racist."

"So you're not sure."

"No."

"Well you might be right. I'm guessin' that many of my brethren in these parts have no idea who Emmett Till was. So they slipped up as far as that goes. They'd done better to go with burning crosses."

"And?"

"And what?"

"You've been edgy all evening, even before this last piece of news. What's going on?"

Cody lit another cigarette. "I don't know. Somethin's makin' me uneasy. I'm not sure what it is. If your dealing with an assassin, that could be it. But I don't think so."

"What then?"

He rubbed his eyes. "I don't know. That's the hardest part. Seein' through the dark glass is worse than not seein' at all. Somethin' bad's ready to move in and I don't know what it is."

"Are you saying the revival's endangering lives?"

"Maybe but I don't think so. I'm guessin' the New York suits could care less about what they'd be callin' a hick revival. The letter may just be their distorted attempt to keep you in your place. I'm not sure. What I do know though is if the WCF had their goons send that letter to you, it's a different matter altogether."

"Why?"

"Because they'd be takin' it personal. And if they think a colored man is jeopardizin' their standing in the world, however twisted, then you'd better look out. They won't be takin' prisoners."

"In that case, I think we'll be okay. The Winston men managing the impoundment are so deep into the pockets of the New York trustees, they won't even sneeze without permission."

"Man I don't know who your sources are, but you seem pretty sure of yourself."

"Look, the people here have a right to assemble and they have a right to begin to take charge of their own lives. That should begin tomorrow."

"I hope it does," Cody said.

They went back inside and Joe headed upstairs to make a few last-minute phone calls before night's end.

Cody sat on the basement couch with his guitar. The room went still except for the rustle of a summer breeze through the window and the moon shadows playing on the wall. These were the moments when he thought about her most often, moments when his mind had room to move and wander and ramble without interruption. Ever since he saw her at the river two years ago, during that brief ethereal encounter when he rose from the baptismal water to see her watching him from the trestle, she increasingly had become seared to his heart. She was his songbird, his Sophia. Sometimes he'd hear her in the far-reaching limbs of his consciousness, invisible but for a faint and distant call. Sometimes he'd find her flitting from branch to branch, oblivious of his presence, dancing and leaping, enthralled in her own joy, amused by the leaves shaken by her folly and raining down upon the ground. Sometimes, when he was quiet and absorbed in his own thinking, she would appear, carefully obscured in her leafy nest, where he would catch a glimpse of her studying him with her head atilt, her expression curious and inquisitive, and when his eyes met hers, she would halt and tremble, and inevitably disappear again into realms unseen.

He marveled at her strength and hard beauty and he ached at her timidity. How much did she know? Could she see him? He hoped so. And he wondered if she could hear him. So he would play his guitar and sing for her as he was doing now, strumming the chords soft and low, wetting a line in her celestial pool, a harmony embracing her melody. *My northern light…afraid of shadow…my winged Cassandra…broken bird…lies in wait…both captor and caged… a tremulous sea…my artesian well…an unyielding flow against the pressing river.*

e%?*

22

Amanda couldn't sleep. Her dreaming had been fitful all week, which was unusual these days. She woke in the middle of the night especially uneasy, with a looming sense of apprehension she couldn't define. It wasn't frightening, not like it used to be; it was more a feeling of anticipation, an impression leaving her senses tuned. To what, she didn't know. She stared at the ceiling for a long time and then finally got out of bed and went outside.

The grass was cool and damp on her bare feet and through the deep shadows she found her way to the backside of the house. She sat down on an old bench and pulled her knees up under her chin. The moon, which had peered into her window only hours before, had vanished completely now. Amanda closed her eyes and relaxed against the night.

Her eyes slowly adjusted to the darkness and she could just make out the wild phantom maneuvers of a small bat lunging and swirling and nipping at unlucky insects on its way back to the barn. Across the field along the ridge, morning teased the horizon, first green then gold blew across the heavens. Soon the sun followed, a ball so red and penetrating that Amanda had to shield her eyes.

She walked down into the garden, thick with the heavy fragrance of dawn. Fans of lettuce stretched out in long rows with strings of dew clinging to their leaves. Large green heads of broccoli stood on fat trunks. Tomato plants bloomed along wire fencing. Pole beans climbed up tall stakes. Mason bees and hummingbirds fought for the nectar pooled in the deep throats of squash flowers and bluebells.

It was Amanda's third growing season and she was getting good at it. Further down the hill, she could see Heidi making her way from the barn toward the lush grasses beckoning from the farthest paddock. Heidi was a runt Guernsey, a gift from Morgan's father who needed to find a home for her because she was too weak for his breeding herds. Her milk was rich and made delicious ice cream and cheese, Amanda discovered. She also managed to reclaim the flock of laying hens that had greeted her on her first day at the farm. The old breeds Bernie had kept were hearty and motherly, and even the last of the old roosters still strutted about the coop displaying his magnificent tail of golden plumes. She loved all of it, more than she ever dreamed she would. The seed and soil, the rhythm of the year, her neighbors' warm and heartfelt acceptance. She felt at home in a way she had never felt at home before.

The phone rang and she sprinted toward the farmhouse.

It was Dehlia calling from the Howard Johnson's to say she was stuck in Fourth of July traffic and was running late, which was no surprise to Amanda. Dehlia always ran late, holiday or no. Amanda was looking forward to seeing her, though. She hadn't been down to visit since winter break. Amanda had talked her into making the trip with news of a music festival taking place in Winston. "Sounds quaint," was Dehlia's response, which made Amanda bristle.

"Quaint? You've got to be kidding," Amanda railed. "What do you think you're coming to see? A freak sideshow? You have no earthly idea what you're talking about. The Roundhouse Revival is a compelling idea, even by the high and mighty standards of the college educated," she added scornfully.

"Okay, okay, I get it. I'm sorry. But don't be looking too closely at my standards. To tell you the truth, I'm thinking of dropping out," she told Amanda. "That is, if I can figure out how to break the news to my parents."

Amanda wasn't completely surprised at the news. Dehlia had

told her about how hard it was. It wasn't a question of competence with Dehlia. She was capable of doing the work; in fact during her first two years, Dehlia had proved a keen and adept scholar. But attitudes were changing on campus especially among the older students who with shocking numbers were leaving school to organize protests or succumbing to the burgeoning variety of contraband permeating the dorms. And Dehlia was not immune. Yet it was not the rallies or the drugs that enticed her; it was the music. She was addicted to it, the poetry, the pounding volume, the audacious and aggressive maelstrom against established thinking. She adored it all and over the course of the year she had skipped countless classes to attend concerts, some in cities miles away. By the end of the semester, she told Amanda, she was put on academic probation.

So Amanda knew she could entice her to come to the Roundhouse Revival. She missed Dehlia and had so much to tell her about the farm. After all, it didn't hurt that the revival promised a heavy dose of local music along with a few national acts that signed on to support the miners who worked along the steep gorge of Blue Ridge coal country.

It was noontime by the time Dehlia arrived. Shortly after that, Morgan's pickup truck could be heard rolling up the driveway. He had ridden to town to pick up Eppy and then circled round to meet up with Amanda and Dehlia at the Yellow Bird where they all planned to head out to the show. "We're over here!" Amanda shouted across the back gate. Morgan opened the door for Eppy and held out his arm so she could hoist herself up and maneuver her enormous belly out of the cab.

"Interesting," Dehlia observed.

"Yes, look at him. Have you ever seen a face so love-struck? The poor boy is head-over-heels."

"But the baby isn't his?"

"Nope, which makes him even more endearing."

"What about Eppy?"

"We haven't talked about it much. As you can see, she's got enough on her mind, and I think she's too afraid right now to believe she could attract a man."

"But he's just about drooling over her," Dehlia said. "And she is a beauty. Ah, so romantic."

"Shhh, they might hear you." Amanda waved them in through the gate and back to the patio.

"I'm not sure I'm gonna make it through the night," Eppy said. "Look at the size of these ankles. They look like tree trunks."

Amanda laughed. "You don't have to if you don't want to. You can ride with me in the Falcon so we can make a quick getaway if need be. Morgan's taking his truck, and Dehlia can follow in her car so she can head straight home from Winston without doubling back. You are taking your truck, aren't you, Morgan?"

"Yeah, got our instruments and amps and stuff in the back. I need to meet my dad and brothers up there before too long, though."

"So you're playing tonight?" Dehlia asked with piqued interest.

Amanda dispensed the introductions. "Morgan and Eppy. This is Dehlia," she said.

"Pleased to meet you," Morgan replied. "Yeah, don't know if we'll still be playing by nightfall. More likely through the afternoon. We was hopin' Eppy would play too, but she don't feel up to it right now." He turned to Eppy. "You think maybe you'd want to sing a little bit, though?"

"What I want and what I can do don't seem to agree anymore, Morgan." Eppy said plopping down on the bench. "I'd like to try but I just don't know. I swear this baby's goin' be a hundred pounds if he's an ounce."

Morgan nodded, "Big and healthy, you can count on that."

"Well, I'd better be on my way," Morgan said. "Nice meetin' you, Dehlia."

"The pleasure's mine," Dehlia said as he left through the gate.

Eppy waved to Morgan then turned toward the sound of a moaning trumpet swelling from inside the bookstore.

"Where's the music comin' from?" Eppy asked.

"Come on, I'll show you." Amanda answered. In front of the store next to the bay window stood a large wooden cabinet with an etched glass panel on the front. "It's an old jukebox I found in the attic in the farmhouse, complete with records."

Eppy ran her hand over the smooth polished wood. "Wow, does it play?"

"Well the coin slots are broken but the rest of it works. Mr. Shelton helped me haul it up here, and he replaced a couple of the belts on the flywheels that move the records to and from the turntable when you press this." She pushed a small white button on the front, and through the glass they watched a metal arm swing gently under the disk and then disappear. Before long, a smooth tenor began to croon "That's My Desire," his voice all smoke and champagne.

"It sounds good," Eppy said.

Amanda pointed to a stack of crates against the wall. "I sorted through all of Bernie's records and these are the ones that weren't either warped or scratched beyond hope. Some date back to before my grandfather died. Check it out." She carefully slipped a 78 recording from its brown sleeve and placed it on the Victrola sitting on a little table against the wall. "My grandfather and Bernie brought this record player back with them from the war." She turned the crank on the side and unlocked the turntable. The maroon OKeh label began to spin and she placed the tonearm on the record. Through the gaping brass horn the record began to crackle, giving way to sloppy trombones and clarinets and finally a woman's strong contralto voice.

"It's Mamie Smith singing 'Let's Agree to Disagree' in the 1920s."

Without a word, Eppy knelt down beside the Victrola. She closed her eyes and listened until the needle traveled the whole length of the disk. "Make me a promise, Amanda," she said.

"All right."

"After I have the baby, promise me that I can bring him here so we can listen to all of Bernie's records anytime we want."

"Him? You think it's a boy?"

"Yes I do. I'm carryin' like it's a boy, and besides, last night, Mamaw and I did the needle test."

"Needle?" Dehlia looked aghast.

"Sure, ever expectin' mama does the needle test. You all ever done it?"

Amanda and Dehlia shrugged.

"That's amazin'. Get me a needle and some thread," she said to Amanda who ran up the stairs, returning with a sewing basket.

"Okay, here we go," Eppy threaded a long embroidery needle

and rolled a knot in the end. "Who wants to go first?"

"You go," Dehlia said, pushing Amanda forward.

"Will it hurt?" Amanda asked.

"Of course not, silly. Give me your hand."

Amanda sat on the floor next to her and stretched out her arm.

"Now hold it real still," she said dangling the thread like a tiny pendulum above the back of Amanda's hand. "Now just wait a minute and watch," she whispered.

They held their breath in rapt attention until ever so slowly the needle began to move. "Hush up," Eppy said, "You've got to focus or it won't work. Now Amanda, you've got to imagine the babies you'll be havin' one day, and the man who's gonna be puttin' them there." Amanda blushed. "See? The needle's startin' to swing in a circle. Yep, plain as day," she smiled. "Looks like you'll be havin' a girl to start." She stopped the needle then let it loose again. "Another girl," she said as the needle circled Amanda's hand. "What d'ya know." Again she stopped the needle and released it.

"It's going back and forth now," Amanda said.

"That's right, third one's a boy." She tried again but the needle hung straight and still.

"Two girls and a boy. That's a nice size family. Who's the lucky man?" Eppy said.

"I don't have a boyfriend," Amanda said.

"I didn't ask that, did I? You can't fool me anyway. I know you're pining over somebody. I've seen that lonesome look you get down in the garden sometimes when you think no one's lookin'. Is he someone from out of town?"

"You might say that."

Dehlia raised her brows.

"I knew it. Well whether you want to admit it or not, he'll be givin' you some beautiful babies. The needle don't lie."

23

Amanda and Eppy pulled into the Maloney farm with Dehlia trailing behind. Men with flags guided them over the field they were using for a parking lot. They ended up having to park further from the attractions than they wanted too. "Guess we should have gotten here earlier," Dehlia said.

"Guess so," Amanda said. "I had no idea there'd be such a turnout."

Eppy blanched at the prospect of hiking clear across the field to the edge of the property where the crowd had gathered at the ticket stalls. "We better get started," she said weakly.

"We'll take our time," Amanda said. "We can stop along the way so you can catch your breath."

In the distance, a whistle blew, two shorts and a long. "It's the No. 49!" Amanda said. "I read where they were running her today to bring people up from the valley. It should pass right behind us in a minute on its way to the Roundhouse."

They leaned against the hood of Amanda's Falcon and waited for the locomotive to appear. From there, they could see all the way across the tracks, over the ridge, and into the coal impoundment below where a sprawling lake was dammed behind it.

"It's huge," Dehlia said.

"Yeah," Amanda agreed, "and getting bigger all the time."

As the old engine approached, the ground began to shake beneath them and the clamor of metal against steel grew deafening as the train pulled up the rail from Twin Gap. The white smoke from its chimney billowed over the trees, signaling its arrival, as did the squeal and hiss of the air brakes as Eugene Gilbert slowed it down. There it was, an outdated 4-4-0 locomotive built in the 1920s. The massive black engine appeared first, and they waved to Mr. Gilbert who let go a brief whistle in reply. Behind the cab was the tender car heaped with wood to feed the cavernous firebox. It was pulling two passenger cars followed by five freights and a red caboose. Eugene guided her to the siding track that ran up to the Roundhouse. Great plumes of steam issued from her every seam as her monstrous form eased to a stop.

When the passengers began to disembark, Amanda, Eppy, and Dehlia headed for the fair grounds too. They hadn't gotten far when a school bus eased up the gravel drive and pulled up alongside of them. The door swung open and a bearded man tipped his cap. "Excuse me, ladies. It's a good long hike to the revival from here, which is why I've been dispatched to help transport the passengers. All aboard," he said lightheartedly guiding them into the seats.

"But we didn't come up on the train," Dehlia confessed. "We drove."

"Half of one, six of another," said the old man. "You gotta use legs either way. We've got a couple seats left." They boarded and Eppy and Dehlia took the last seat behind the driver and Amanda stood. "Hold on, it's a bumpy ride," he said as the bus bounded toward the fair grounds.

Amanda and Dehlia jumped out as soon as the doors opened, but Eppy stayed in her seat talking to the driver until everyone had filed out. Then the old man crept down the steps and held out his hand to help Eppy navigate the stairs.

Eppy joined them in the ticket line. "Can you believe it? He knows my daddy. Turns out they worked together years ago at the Herston office when my father was just startin' out. He's been retired from the railroad for about ten years but likes to help Mr. Gilbert run the 49 when he can."

Dehlia looked at Amanda. "Eppy has a gift," Amanda explained, "which constitutes being able to draw every bit of news or gossip out of anybody at any time for any reason. She got it from her grandmother, Mary Lynn, whom you've yet to have the privilege of meeting."

They paid their money and got their hands stamped and then fought their way through the crowd to see which way to go. Along the perimeter to their right were the food stands. The Lions Club had rows of grills covered with burgers, hotdogs, and toasted buns. The Ladies Auxiliary sponsored the bake sale, and mountains of coconut cakes, chess pies, and lemon meringue were perched precariously along checkered cloth tables. The Boy Scouts sold drinks a quarter apiece – Pepsi, Dr. Pepper, Nehi.

A huge tent sprawled across the back of the grounds where a variety of seminars were taking place. The Red Cross had posted the schedule out front and Amanda, Dehlia, and Eppy read the itinerary while licking their frozen custard cones.

"Looks like we missed the emergency preparedness exercise," Dehlia said.

"Anyone up for first aid basics?" Amanda asked.

Eppy laughed. "You might wish you'd taken it if I should decide to have this child right here tonight."

"That's not funny, Eppy," Amanda said tossing her cone into the trash. She walked over to a small clearing in the center of the fair where she could hear the band warming up. She watched while they began a sound check and a loud peal of feedback echoed in her ears. Suddenly she felt cold all over and began to tremble uncontrollably. Dehlia saw her and motioned to Eppy.

"Is she havin' one of her fits?" Eppy whispered.

"You mean you've seen them too? I thought she was over them."

"They've not been so bad lately. Ever once in a while, though, she seems to give in to one." Eppy took Amanda by the arm. "You okay?"

Amanda nodded. "Who is that man?" she asked.

"What man?" Eppy asked craning her neck.

"The one that just passed us. Right there. Baseball cap and tee shirt."

"Good God almighty, Amanda. You've just pegged about every man here. Who in the world are you talkin' about?"

"That one," she pointed. "The one with the alligator tattoo on his forearm."

"Who? Oh, now I see him."

"Do you know who that is?"

"No, but remember I'm from Glen Mills. Morgan might know him. Why?"

"Because she thinks he's the devil," Dehlia interjected. "Isn't that right, Amanda? You think that guy is who triggered your trip to never neverland this time. I'm right, admit it."

"Oh, shut up. I don't know what's going on, but I know there's something awfully wrong about that man being here. He's trouble. I'm sure of it." Amanda got up. "I'm going to follow him."

"Hold on there just a minute," Eppy said pulling her back. "You ain't goin' nowhere without me. And I can't risk waltzin' into a crowd like that. Dear God in heaven, how would I ever get back out if my water broke?"

"I'll go," Dehlia said. "I always like to get as close as I can to the stage anyway. What kind of weirdo is this guy, Amanda?"

"I don't know. Maybe it's nothing, but still…"

"Here, finish this." She handed Amanda her ice cream and she wove her way through the crowd.

Amanda and Eppy turned their attention to the activity on the stage.

Tonk, tonk, tonk, thumped through the speakers. A black man stood on the stage tapping the mic.

"Who's that?" Eppy asked.

"I don't know."

"May I have your attention please?" Joe said. He was wearing a gray suit, and the white of his shirt collar accentuated his dark and serious features. "We hope everyone is enjoying the first annual Roundhouse Revival. We're happy to see so many of you here today. Before we begin the music portion of our program, I'd like to acknowledge the many hardworking citizens of Porterstown, Twin Gap, and Winston who made this event possible." He paused to slip a pair of horn-rimmed glasses from his coat pocket.

"What's he doing?" Amanda asked. "Why's he stopping? Is something wrong?"

"Would you relax? You're makin' me nervous. It's hard to see from here but there's not a thing wrong as far as I can tell."

Amanda covered her eyes. Her heart began to race and she found it hard to breath.

"What on earth is wrong with you? Come on, let's go over here." Eppy led them to a grassy patch next to a split rail fence.

They sat down on the ground and Amanda rested her head on her bent knees. All she could see in her mind's eye was that strange man and his alligator tattoo. With her eyes closed she could see the blue and red of his tattoo and it began to squirm and pulse along his arm. The thing grew and twisted and uncoiled. Distorted and writhing, it slowly opened its gaping jaws, an enormous spiked cavern. A glassy reptile eye appeared through its scaly fold and stared at her. It raised it head, poised to strike. She froze and then she screamed.

A sound from the stage broke her trance. "Excuse me, Reverend," came the voice across the loud speakers. Amanda looked up. A figure, hard to distinguish at that distance, had taken the mic. She blinked once, then twice, to determine if she was still dreaming. It was a man, his white face only a blur of features. "I don't mean to interrupt," he said, his voice low and mellow. "Well actually I suppose I do mean to interrupt." Soft laughter swelled from the gathering audience. "Before we go further with the formalities, I wanted to remind our fine citizens to smile broad and wide. That's right, say hello to Sammy Wright and his crew." He pointed to Sammy in the wings. "These talented fellows will be filming today's events in living color. Bring your camera out here, Sammy, so they can see it." He waved him onto the stage to a small rise of applause. "That's good, very good. Now Reverend, if I might dare to change up the rundown a little," Cody continued. "I just got word that the July sun is wreakin' havoc on the baked goods table, and Mrs. Jenkins of the Ladies Auxiliary would greatly appreciate it if we would commence with the cake raffle straight away. Is that okay with you?" Joe waved him on. "Well then, Anna, will you be so kind as to come on stage."

From the wings came Anna Jenkins holding a large fishbowl filled with raffle tickets. "Thank you. Now, we need a volunteer from the audience to help us select a winner. Who will it be?" A hundred hands shot up from the crowd. "Let's see. So hard to choose from such a fine lookin' crowd. What'ya think, Mrs. Jenkins. Who will it be?" Hands waved and the people whooped. Anna shrugged. "Sammy, get in real close so they'll be no mistake. Takes a lucky hand to pick the right ticket." Cody took the mic off the stand and paced along the edge of the stage. "Who will it be? Nope, not you," he said scanning the faces. Awww from the amused crowd. "Nope I don't think so, not quite right." Then he slowly tiptoed to center stage and spun around.

"You, right there," he said pointing into the crowd. "That's right, you. Alligator Man. Come on up," The man shook his head, trying to back into the crowd. "Hold it right there, mister. I'm sure you wouldn't want to disappoint our distinguished guests. Ain't that right, ladies and gentlemen. Sammy, you getting' this? Who among you would like to see our very own Roundhouse Revival Alligator Man." The crowd roared. "Please help our lucky volunteer to the stage," Cody said as the man was seized and carried up.

Amanda laughed. Her panic defused as quickly as it had flared, and she wiped tears from her wet face. That voice, it resonated to her core and lingered. Who is that? While the reverend stepped forward to finish his introductions, she remained enamored, her mind drifting about in its own relief, contemplating his tone and timbre, puzzled at the way he made her feel. Before she knew it, the music began. That voice again, only singing, picking a guitar. The simplicity of it was shattering in its authenticity. The sound, the cadence, the breath, plumbing down down down through the ages, drawing up the culmination of memory. A telescopic ballad, collapsing all that we know against all that we want, stirring that part of the soul that has lain sleeping for so very long.

24

"How are you holding up?" Amanda asked as she turned out of the parking lot onto the road south towards home.

"Not so good," Eppy said, riding shotgun and slumped back in the seat as far as she could.

The rain was coming down hard now, and even though it was not yet dusk, Amanda needed the headlights to help her see down the road. "You should have said something, Eppy. We stayed way too long."

Eppy only nodded with her eyes closed, her hands on her belly. The wipers swept sheets of water off the windshield beating wildly to keep up with the torrent. "Too bad the weather didn't hold for a little while longer. People were having such a good time," Amanda said. "At least we got out ahead of the crowd."

They rode in silence the rest of the way and as they approached the farmhouse, she saw that a wide pool of water had collected across the road. "It's all or nothing, seems like," Amanda said. "First a dry spell to bake the ground to brick, and now this. Should I try and clear it?"

"Just drive, Amanda. If I don't take a pee real soon, I won't care if we cross it or not."

She barreled straight through and turned hard into the driveway bouncing and splashing around the curves. The Falcon slid to a stop in front of the house and moaned when she turned off the engine. Eppy threw open the door and held out her arms so Amanda could pull her up. "He's turnin' somersaults like a circus clown," she said. "It'll be a miracle if I don't wet my pants before we get inside." As they made their way to the porch, Amanda noticed the dark circles gaining ground under Eppy's eyes. "Good God, we look like drowned rats," Eppy said. "You got somethin' dry you think I can fit into?"

"Yeah, there's a couple of nightgowns in the bedroom. One of those ought to be big enough. Go ahead and change. I'll call Mary Lynn and let her know you'll be spending the night."

"Thanks, I think it's best. No way I'm goin' back out there until it clears up. I'll get some towels too," she said as she shuffled towards the bedroom.

Mary Lynn barked into the phone when she heard Amanda's voice. "I told you, you all had no business goin' to the revival, especially with Eppy in the state she's in, and look what happened. You should be thankin' your lucky stars that you got back at all," she was both angry and relieved. "It's no better down here, that's for sure. I got buckets catchin' drips all over this diner and still the water's findin' new holes." After she cooled down, she began to ask about all that had happened: the speakers, the seminars, the food, the music, and she was particularly probing about the tours along the ridge.

"It was fantastic," Amanda told her. "There it was, in all its glory, exposed for all to see. You could see the WCF pacing around the impoundment down there and sweating bullets, not being able to do a thing about it, since we were all standing on Mrs. Mahoney's property."

Mary Lynn's broad smile could be felt right through the phone line. "It's about time someone stood up to them. A bunch of blowhards up there, that's what they are, without the sense to know they're no more than pawns for their all-important New York bigwigs. They think we're stupid, but we can read a newspaper as good as anyone. And besides our men who work the mines can see exactly what's goin' on. The WCF thinks it's gettin' away with murder up there, on the backs of all of us. Well we'll just see about that."

"I'm sorry you didn't come up there with us," Amanda said, averting the oncoming diatribe. "You would have loved the train."

"Are you kiddin'? You think for a minute I'd put my life in the hands of Mr. Eugene Gilbert who no doubt crossed that old worn-down trestle even in all this slop. No sir, not me. Besides those that didn't go were countin' on me keepin' the diner open. We had a good show for dinner, fewer for supper. I may as well close up now though. Nobody in their right mind will be coming out in this weather." Amanda could hear her clearing dishes while she talked. "Have you called your mother?"

"Yeah, before I called you. It's hot and dry in Chicago. She seems happy enough up there. I told her I'd call her again tomorrow after the rain lets up."

When Amanda got off the phone, she put a pot of soup on the stove and went to change her clothes. She heard Eppy groan as she flopped into Bernie's big overstuffed chair and then sigh after hauling her legs onto the wide hassock. "It feels like heaven," Eppy murmured sinking her head into the cushion. She looked like a porcelain doll: the billowing flannel gown that hid her swollen belly, her legs spread comfortably, her toes pointed up in stocking feet, her damp hair falling in soft copper locks over her shoulders, her face, once rosy and flushed, now smooth and white as ivory. Only the telling bend in her otherwise straight brow and the firm set of her pale lips hinted at the weight of motherhood pressing hard upon her.

Amanda was setting up trays for dinner when the lights went out, which was not uncommon in Twin Gap. "Good thing the soup's hot already," she said as she went about the room lighting candles. "Here you go. It's chicken noodle." She set a steaming bowl in front of Eppy along with a chunk of bread and some soft cheese. "There's not much to drink, either water or milk. Come to think of it, we won't have water until the pump comes back on so I'll get us some milk."

"You think Morgan's made it back yet?" Eppy asked.

"I hope so. The phone's still working so why don't you call him? I'll see if the cord will reach that far." Amanda dragged the phone over and Eppy placed it between her legs. She tucked the receiver under her chin and dialed. "Morgan? It's Eppy."

Amanda was hungrier than she thought and devoured her meal. She got up to get more and looked out the window. The rain continued to cut through the night in great silver sheets blowing through the trees and pounding the ground. The rain barrels under the downspouts spewed geysers that leaped up and over their rims. It would have been beautiful to behold if she was not still bothered by a troubling uneasiness.

Since her baptism at the trestle, the haunting abyss that was her old world had disappeared. How it happened, she didn't quite understand; nevertheless, on that singular day, she had landed on new ground; a seedbed upon an endless void, which in its own time, bloomed into a living firmament; it was a beating heart; a mystical womb. Where once she had lived in profound isolation, she now abided in a refuge as alive as the fertile earth, not made of flesh and blood, yet more real than anything she had ever known. Since that day of reckoning, she began a quiet exploration of her new world, first a practiced and deliberate attention to the remarkable gift given her, then an evermore penetrating recognition of the presence that both breathed the air she breathed and was the air she breathed. Her brain let go of its old and harmful courses, gratefully succumbing to the cognitive awareness sprouting from her soul, a language new to her but ancient and eternal in its address, a mythical hand to hold, a friend unseen but intimately known who would guide her wherever her life would take her now.

How does one explain? One doesn't, Amanda decided. It was impossible to put into words, so she would continue her journey in silence, her friends and family content with the simple explanation that she was a happier person. Looking out into the sodden night, from the light of her new world, it was her uneasiness that was commanding her attention now. Once Eppy went to bed she would sit in counsel and wait.

"Morgan got back okay," Eppy said hanging up the phone, "but all their instruments and equipment got drenched before they could get 'em in the truck. He said there's lots of standin' water on all the roads. He's headin' down to the barn next to make sure all the calving cows made it back." She started to laugh.

"What so funny about that?"

"Nothin', it's what he told me about Dehlia. Remember all your frettin' over the Alligator Man. Well turns out you were onto somethin'. Morgan was standin' backstage when Reverend Price began to speak, and clean out of nowhere, this guy nearly knocks him down to get on stage. Morgan said his name was Cody Stone, some guy from Rocky Creek, who has been playin' guitar with the Jenkins Country Band now and then. Before he grabbed the microphone from the reverend, he signaled to a guy named Danny to get on his radio. Suddenly without askin' no one, this guy Cody starts into his act, the one we saw when he began pumpin' up the crowd for the cake raffle." Eppy dipped her bread into the soup and took a bite. She licked her fingers and continued.

"Well turns out it was all a charade. Somehow, and Morgan didn't know how, this Cody Stone suspected someone in the crowd was going to harm the reverend so he got in the way while they figured out who it was. And wouldn't you know, Dehlia was the one who drew attention to the Alligator Man. Morgan said she kept bumpin' into him and holding onto his alligator arm all the way up to the front of the crowd and still she didn't let up. That's when they singled him out and made him get on stage. All the while they got him on film, which was the plan from the start, to get everything on film. After the reverend took the mic again, they whisked the Alligator Man off to where Officer Denfield was waitin' for him. Turns out the man had a gun! Can you believe it?" she said slapping her knee. "A gun! So you were right about him all along. He must've been out to kill somebody to take a firearm into the fair." She put her bowl on the end table and leaned back into the cushion again.

"The funny part is that they took Dehlia in for questionin' too thinking she was the Alligator Man's girlfriend. Morgan had to come down to the station to convince them that Dehlia had actually been with us and that she and the Alligator Man were strangers. Can you just see it?" Eppy roared, wiping the tears from her eyes.

As the story unfolded Amanda was at first pierced by the realization that Reverend Price had been within a hair of being shot. But as Eppy continued, and the tale flew from impending tragedy to a safe haven where the reverend was somehow spared, she laughed too, partly out of relief, partly at picturing Dehlia explaining her way out of yet another absurd predicament.

The room settled into a comfortable glow of candlelight, and with a full stomach, dry clothes, and a lighter heart, Eppy soon excused herself and went to bed. Amanda lit some kindling in the fireplace, as much for company as for a balm against the dampening air. As the flames rose gently up the chimney, her thinking hovered over the day's events as well as the knot that tightened around her apprehension. And there, in the periphery of her deepening meditation, was Gabriel.

25

Cody was up before dawn smoking in the open freight car
and listening to the radio while the rain continued to pour. Trees
were beginning to topple onto electric lines, too heavy for the water-
laden soil. Power was out in Twin Gap and half of Porterstown. The
local station reported that the city councilmen had just cancelled the
Fourth of July festivities to the profound chagrin of the townspeople
who had marched in the parade down Main Street without fail for as
long as anyone could remember.

Last night, Cody had ridden the old 49 from Winston to Porterstown with Eugene, Walter, Danny, and a hundred drenched passengers anxious to get back home. Danny invited Cody to stay over at
his apartment, but he declined. There was something about the train
that drew him in and Eugene, who understood its allure better than
anyone, saw no harm in letting him spend the night there.

Cody lit another cigarette and his mind turned to thoughts of
the revival. How had she known which man had carried the gun? He
remembered being backstage tuning up when he suddenly became
aware of her panic, when he could feel her racing heart. Even after all
this time, he still never knew exactly where she was, or whether she
inhabited this earth or realms beyond. But he could see her, nonethe-
less, and he could stand by her and comfort her, and there was noth-

ing in this world or the next that could keep him from doing it. He was destined to be with her, he knew that now. But he was getting tired, and he began to wonder if all he would ever be permitted were these veiled and elusive encounters. A single shining thread is all that held them together, a fragile line spun from fate's implacable web, meager scraps of truth, strewn and indecipherable, exhausting his heart and eroding his faith.

He tossed the butt of his cigarette into the rain and watched it etch a wide arch before it was snuffed out on the wet ground. He couldn't explain how it happened, but it did happen. He had seen her tremble at the sight of the stranger entering the revival grounds, he had felt her shudder when she saw the man's tattoo. He knew he was seeing what she was seeing: the dragon come alive. Coiling and snapping and then charging. Clamping its distorted gargantuan jaws over the stage reducing it to shards and splinters.

"Hey man, we've been lookin' all over for you," Danny said, his head peering into the freight car. "Thought you'd be havin' breakfast with everybody else. What'ya doing out here?"

"Watchin' it rain."

"Well you gonna eat or not? Wayne's not likely to ask you twice." Cody hopped down and as they approached the dining car, they could smell the hot grease and burnt toast.

Inside behind the tight counter, Wayne plated both of them three fried eggs, grits, and a thick slab of salty ham. "Coffee's on the table," he grumbled, turning again to his grill.

They joined Eugene who was pouring sugar in his mug when his radio sounded. "Devil Dog, this is Rum Runner, do you copy?" crackled a man's voice through the speaker.

Eugene grabbed the handset. "This is Devil Dog. Have they made a decision yet? Over."

"No but it doesn't look good. Brakeman says the track up around Fort Henry bridge is likely to wash out if this keeps up. He's waitin' to hear from the others, but nothin's leavin' Herston right now, that's for sure. Over."

"I was afraid of that. Keep me posted. Devil Dog, Out." He leaned on the table and stared out the window, the lines deepening in his face.

"Doesn't sound good," Cody said.

"Nope, not good at all," Eugene said. "I'll be back. I've got a few calls to make." He grabbed the radio and walked into the next car.

"What's goin' on?" Danny asked.

"Eugene wants me to fire her up," Wayne said through a mouthful of grits. "But it's gonna take longer with the wood so wet. I'll need your help."

"Why are you runnin' the 49?" Danny asked. "The holiday parade's been called off. You got something special to haul?"

Wayne pulled away from the table. "I don't know. Best to wait on Eugene. In the meantime, we need to get started."

Cody was standing in the tender tossing wood through the bunker when Wayne called to him from the cab. "That'll do for now. Come on down. Eugene wants a word with us."

Cody stripped off his rain gear and laid it in the cab near the firebox to dry then joined the other men in the dining car. Eugene was grave. Cody knew him well enough to know that beneath his stony features was a mind fighting hard to reconcile what to tell them. "Keep these on you at all times," he said, handing them each a radio. "Extra batteries are in the cab. I hope you all slept sound last night. It's likely to be the last we get for awhile."

He'd been in touch with dispatch at the south end of the line down at Herston. The track just north of Hazelton has washed out. It would get worse before it got better. Because of the holiday schedule, all the trains were stationed south of the breach. Nothing would be running up the line to Porterstown or points north today or anytime soon. "Folks around here will just have to stay put," he said. He warmed up his coffee. "I also talked to Bill up in Winston." He looked over at Cody. "You know that cameraman you and the reverend brought down here?"

"Yeah, his name is Sammy," Cody said.

"Well he's been up to the widow's field and was creeping along the ridge above the impoundment to start up his camera. He told Bill it's like an anthill over there. The WCF bosses and what looks like to him a bunch of other drones are runnin' around with hard hats and clipboards, hollerin' into their radios. He said he saw a small copter appear over the mountain comin' from the West Virginia side, like it was tryin' to land out there around Pond 3, but it kept getting' knocked around by the rain hammerin' down and the gale wind blowin' through the gap. So it finally gave up and took off."

The silence that followed was searing. Finally Eugene continued. "The reverend left to go up there the minute he heard and he told Sammy to keep the camera rolling if he could." He tapped his fingers on the table. "It's bad. Real bad. Bill said it could blow."

Cody finally asked what no one else could bring themselves to ask. "You mean the impoundment?"

"Yes."

"A flood."

"Yes."

For Cody, it was the moment when everything began to drag; dark metal weights pulling hard on any sense of time and space making him feel like he was in a dream. He wanted to run but his legs betrayed him, he wanted to scream but his open mouth was silent.

26

Eppy hung up the phone. "Mamaw said I'd do best to stay up here. Hope you don't mind the company."

"What's going on in Porterstown?"

Eppy sat down at the kitchen table. "The diner's full of water. She couldn't keep up with the bailin' so it's runnin' all over the floor. The creek behind the house is startin' to overflow its banks. The wind is whipping everything to pieces. Mrs. Kincaid told her that those in the Red Cross that didn't drive out earlier this mornin' were stuck there in Porterstown since no trains were coming through. They're settin' up cots in the fire hall for themselves and anyone else that might need a place to stay. She said the families along the river have water up to their sidewalks already. But it looks like the rain's lettin' up a little, so they're hopin' they've reached the end of it." She looked up. "Amanda? Amanda, what's wrong with you? You haven't heard a word I said."

Amanda was looking out the back door. The rain had in fact slowed and the clouds appeared to be thinning. Even so, the water spilled over the lawn and down the driveway deepening the rills it had carved in the soil over the last two days. She picked up the phone to call her mother. The line was dead. "Phone's out," is all she said.

"Anybody home?" came Morgan's voice through the front door.

Eppy brightened. "Where else would we be?"

He wiped the mud off his shoes, let himself in, and found them in the kitchen. "Thought I'd come over before it gets dark or rains more. I can't believe so much water can be holed up in the sky. I was glad to hear you all made it home okay yesterday," he said looking at Eppy and flushing. "There's no more my brothers and me can do for Pop just now so I've come to see if Amanda needs any help."

"Thanks, Morgan," Amanda said. "You're a mind reader. I was just thinking about going down to the barn to check on the animals. It'd be a big help if you'd come with me." She stepped into the mud-room and put on her slicker and boots. "After we get back, why don't you stay for dinner? I'm serving the last of anything in the fridge. If the power doesn't come back on soon, it'll all be spoiled anyway."

"Sounds like a feast."

"Wake me up when you get back," Eppy said. "I've got to lay down awhile. I'm whupped."

Amanda and Morgan leaned into the wind as they walked the path from the house to the old barn. It was a stalwart building with planks as hard as iron weathered by countless storms that had blown through the gap over the long years. Amanda pulled on the barn's huge sliding door. "It won't budge," she said, pointing to the runners buried in thick mud. "Let's go down around back."

Their boots made sucking sounds as they tramped down the slope around to where the barn's stone foundation banked into the hill. When they rounded the corner, a sharp gust hit them hard knocking Amanda down. Morgan held out his hand and hoisted her up. She could hear Heidi swishing around in her stall and was relieved to know she had made her way up from the pasture. "You think she'll be all right standing in all this muck?" Amanda stroked the cow's broad flank.

They were standing ankle-deep in water. "She seems content enough and it ain't cold. She'll be fine." He craned his neck to get a good look at the buttresses soaring two stories above them. "Want me to climb up there to see if the hay's gettin' wet?"

"I'll go." She started up the ladder to the loft and heard a loud wailing sound. "What's that?"

"I don't know. Sounds like a siren."

27

Cody was sitting with Eugene when the call came through.

"Breaker, breaker. Blue Jay to Devil Dog. Mayday. Do you copy? Mayday!" the tension in Bill's voice was unmistakable.

"Blue Jay, this is Devil Dog. I hear you. What's your situation? Over."

"Mayday. Sound the whistle and don't let her stop. WCF set off the alarm. Reverend says water's crestin' over Pond 2 and the west side's becoming dangerous. Over."

Eugene signaled to Wayne who jumped up and ran to the cab. "Will it hold? Over."

"They don't know but it don't look good. Over."

Wayne sounded two shorts from the 49 then tied the whistle down wide open. The screaming alarm was strong and continuous, resonating down Main Street and through to the neighboring hollows of Porterstown.

"What about Herston?" Eugene asked. "You get any word about help from down there? Over."

"They got crews workin' on the tracks but it's a mess. There ain't no trains north of the breach." The pause strained over the radio waves. Bill cleared his throat. "The 49's all we got. Get the people to higher ground any way you can. Out."

28

Mary Lynn ran out of the diner when she heard the alarm. It was the old 49. The rain had stopped leaving behind gale winds stirred up by the sudden change in air pressure. Garbage cans, old tarps, newspaper, and every sort of debris not battened down swept through alleys and over roads. People were leaving their porches and milling around in the streets, bracing against gusts that blew in every direction. Children excited by the flurry splashed through puddles and leaped into the newly formed pools on their front lawns.

Suddenly the siren at the firehouse blared overhead. Everyone turned toward as the fire and rescue truck pulled out of the station blinking its blue and red lights. Mary Lynn dashed back inside the diner. "There's a fire or somethin'," she hollered to the handful of regulars she'd been serving from the little she had left in the pantry. "We gotta get out. Now!" She flew into the kitchen. "Virgil, that means you too. Get out. I'm closin' up." She shooed everyone out the door and they joined the swelling crowd gathered now on town square.

Cody and Danny had run the few blocks from Porterstown station and pressed through swarms of people to get to the steps of town hall where they could see Mrs. Mahoney holding a bullhorn and flipping pages on a clipboard, speaking intently to the remaining Red Cross volunteers. When they reached her, Cody stepped back and let Danny do the talking. As Danny laid out Eugene's instructions, the women huddled close around him, and Cody could see Mrs. Mahoney nodding earnestly at every word.

Finally Mrs. Mahoney emerged at the top of the steps of town hall. "Listen up, people!" she shouted through the bullhorn. "It is by God's good graces that we were given our instructions just yesterday at the Roundhouse Revival. We must move quickly. That much we know. There's word from Winston. Hear me now!" The bullhorn's feedback squealed through the crowd. "Listen up! We are in grave danger. They say the dam may go."

A complete and sudden hush consumed the stricken crowd, a spontaneous recognition of their collective nightmare. "I remind you," she continued. "We can thank God we are prepared for this. But we must act quickly and we must act calmly. We have one hour to evacuate. I repeat. One hour. Use the flyers we're handin' out. Pack what's on the list. There's no time for laggin'. Most all the roads out of town are washed out or underwater. Those that intended to be leavin' by car may have trouble gettin' out. And it's gettin' worse by the minute." She pointed to a man in emergency gear waving his hand. "If you still want to take your chances drivin', meet over there. Ricky will tell you if there are any roads left to higher ground. The rest of you must meet back here in one hour. I repeat. One hour, not a minute more. At six p.m. sharp the 49 leaves for Winston."

29

Cody and Danny had just returned to the train when their radios sounded. It was Sammy calling Bill from the ridge. "Joe's gone down to WCF headquarters. We got a call from New York. Apparently the helicopter attempt yesterday was the National Guard. When they failed to land, they set down in a clearing over the mountain and hiked in. Our team was able to patch them through to Joe. Joe told them the scope of the situation in Porterstown and Twin Gap. He got the Guard to allow him in. They've run a line over Pond 2 and the impoundment. I saw them towing a lifeboat along it to rescue a few men who got stranded on our side where the water is lurching up and cutting into the bank. Joe got there in time to cross over with them. He told me to call you and say they've alerted the state and county disaster relief offices. But it's blowing like hell up here so I doubt they'll be able to fly in. Joe says the roads across the mountain are in bad shape too. Copy?

"Roger. Evacuation is in progress in Porterstown. The 49 will be pulling out any minute. We've got to get everyone out before nightfall. Sammy, if you're a prayin' man, now's the time. Blue Jay, Out."

30

Amanda and Morgan heard sirens coming from both directions. "What on earth is going on?" Amanda said, climbing from the top of the ladder into the mow.

"Beats me. I never heard nothin' like that."

"Everything's fine up here. Let's get back to the house. We might hear something on the radio, unless my batteries are dead." She started back down when a deafening explosion rattled the barn and nearly threw her off the ladder. "Morgan!" The noise was savage and roared and swelled to a thunderous pitch. It was an unearthly sound, pounding, scrapping, cracking, grinding, and then another blast.

Heidi's eyes widened and she ran out of the barn. Morgan looked down. The water was rising and quickly covered his knees. "Get back up there," he shouted, pressing through the rising tide. By the time he reached the ladder the water had cleared his waist. He scrambled up the rungs, his pants covered in black silt. Amanda helped him over the top and he fell in a mound of hay to catch his breath. By the time he thought of Eppy, Amanda was already pulling at the sliding door trying to get out.

"It's still stuck." She screamed to be heard over the roar. Water began to seep up and over the floorboards. She threw open the window. "Eppy! Eppy!" They shouted her name as loud as they could hoping she could hear them over the wrenching thunder.

Finally Eppy appeared at the door still half asleep. Water was rising over the porch and creeping into the house. Morgan called to her and then climbed out the window. "Eppy, stay right where you are. I'm comin' over there." He barely reached the wide drive between them when another explosion shook the ground. Amanda ran to the window on the north side, and all at once she saw it as it passed. Beyond her property where the Chalahume River cut through the gap, great frothing billows of white smoke rose over the ravine and filled the sky. Another blast sounded and the smoke gave way to a hideous wall of black water thirty feet tall, high enough to fill the gap and still rush up and over its steep banks pounding onto her farm as it passed.

Water flashed over the fields and into the barn's lower floor inundating it instantly. Outside where the second floor met the driveway, Morgan was still trying to cross over to the house. A river began to take form, whirling and spinning, first in one direction then another. He lost his footing and splashed headlong into its pelting froth. Then all at once, with uncanny swiftness, the torrents calmed, and what moments before had been a raging river now became a sinister lake engulfing half the barn and the house up to its sills. Morgan stood waist deep, fighting not the current now but the unyielding wind that whipped at his face and hands. A quarter mile up the steep path, the bookstore sat untouched.

"Get upstairs, hurry up!" he hollered to Eppy and she disappeared into the house. Just as the words left his mouth another explosion rattled the ground. Again the river formed, the quiet surface belying a ferocious undertow.

Floodwater sped into the mow with unbelievable force and Amanda struggled to reach the rough dilapidated ladder nailed to the barn wall. She looked up and saw that it led to a hatch in the metal roof twenty feet above her. She began to climb. And climb and climb. Now her sense of what was real left her and although her feet appeared to be stepping on rung after rung, she didn't know if she was moving. She stopped to regain her balance, to close her eyes and find the anchor in her soul that so often saved her. Almost immediately, a steady force pushed her from within and she climbed again, over rot-

ted slats and bent nails until she reached the top. Wind blew relentlessly through the cracks in the small door and it rattled and banged
against the latch. She pulled on the rusty clasp but it wouldn't budge.
She tried again as water closed in. At the last moment before panic
completely overtook her, she slammed her fist into the hatch. It burst
open, tearing from its sash and was carried off by the wind. Her hand
ached and throbbed but she managed to crawl through the opening
and onto the barn roof.

The view from the rooftop was unforgiving. From her high
perch, Amanda saw all of her gardens and pastures buried in the
black tide, sinking deeper and deeper where they sloped toward the
gap. Downriver the destruction was fast and fierce. As the floodwall
thrust itself through the gorge, the rocky cliffs took the brunt of its
brute force. Everything in its immediate path simply disappeared.
Huge trees were plucked effortlessly from their roots. Telephone
poles, boulders, sheds, animals, all gone in an instant. She also saw
what her mind would not accept. She saw people. Swept from the
crumbling banks and pulled under. Gone. And she knew in a matter
of moments, the beast would reach what was just barely out of her
line of sight: the old trestle at Twin Gap.

"Morgan!" It was Eppy shouting through the attic window. He
was almost to the porch when a log swept by and knocked him down.
He struggled against the undertow that pulled on his legs and he
clawed the front door searching for a handhold. He found the door-
knob and turned it. A gush of water spewed out the door and it flung
wide open. He slammed against the wall and the door closed again.
Back and forth it creaked and strained battling the contrary winds
and beating tides with Morgan holding fast. With a loud crack, the
door burst from its hinges, first going airborne then landing flat on
the whirling waves with Morgan firmly astride. He held tight as his
raft gained speed and sailed down the driveway and out of sight.

31

By dusk, Porterstown was deserted, the evacuation complete. Or so they thought. Unbeknownst to the firemen and police who swept through every building they could, there were a few lone souls who chose to stay on and hide out, hoping to go unnoticed as the town struggled through utter angst and confusion while attempting to board the train to safety.

Finally the old 49 pulled out of the station and groaned against the incline as it strained up the hill toward Twin Gap. The tracks were holding so far as anyone knew, and with every passing moment they were that much closer to the safe haven of higher ground. The train was packed. The children, the elderly, and the infirm rode in the passenger cars. Those who could stand did so shoulder-to-shoulder. The ablest men climbed on top of the cars or helped in the tender and cab. The rest crammed into the freight cars.

The neon sign over the Silver Goose Diner wasn't flashing now, dead since the power went out the night before. The diner itself was dark but for a single candle glowing through the window. Mary Lynn watched the red light of the caboose shrink slowly in the distance and then disappear around the bend. "Don't you worry about me, Henry. After all, it was you who said there are worse things than dyin'." She caressed the gold frame that held her husband's image.

"I've missed you terribly all these years, Henry. But I've done all right for myself." She picked up the photo and smiled. "I know, I know. I shouldn't have hid. But I had to. You see, there was no gettin' around it. How could I up and leave, Henry? You know me better than that. My life is right here," she said patting the table. "Oh don't worry, I'm a tough old bird now. You should see me, all wrinkles and sags," she laughed softly. "They say it's goin' to go. Yep. Can you believe it's been all these years since it took you?" She shook her head. "How's that possible? No, Henry. I haven't forgotten. All things is possible to those who love God. Truth is, my love, I'm tired of this world, real tired. Henry, I want to go home."

32

The 49 crept up the measured grade, its formidable carriage grinding metal on metal. They hadn't gotten far from the Porterstown station when Eugene saw people coming out of nowhere, clambering from roofs, jumping out of flooded cars, climbing up the gap's eroding mountain paths, all in a frenzy to reach the train before it passed. Thirty feet below the track, the Chalahume churned black and frothy and wind-whipped, but what puzzled Eugene was the fact that the river wasn't running any higher than earlier in the day.

Cody and Danny were in the tender throwing wood down the bunker to Wayne who was feeding the firebox. Over the driving wind, Cody heard the screams of people struggling to pull their family aboard, and he heard the cries of those who were unsuccessful. As the train advanced, so did the amount of flotsam in the water. First trees and stumps, then cars, refrigerators, furniture. And yet the river didn't rise. It rushed through the gap in a torrent but there was no flood. It made no sense. His mind began to lock up. The people moaning, the explosions he heard moments ago, and now a huge cloud of smoke pressing through the gorge. It brought back what he had put away a long time ago: thoughts of the war, the village, the children. The dead children.

"Come on, man. This is no time to quit," he heard Danny say, but the words sounded distorted, like he was talking through molasses. Cody stared and couldn't move. When he sat down, he heard Danny again, but only barely. "Wayne, send somebody up here to help. Jeremiah's about to pass out."

He knew he'd see her and he did. She was a yellow bird perched high in her cathedral sky. He thought she should be singing as birds do when freed from the earth's pull. But no. She wasn't happy. She was terrified. He saw her green eyes frozen in a stare. He saw the farmhouse and he saw the water. Then the house turned to glass, an enormous fishbowl with water pouring in and in and up and up. But then he saw it wasn't a fishbowl after all. Now he could see that it was a tomb.

He woke up as they approached Twin Gap. In the dimming light of day, he climbed to the other side of the tender, and unseen by anyone, he stood on the edge and jumped off.

⁊

33

As the engine neared Twin Gap, the trees gave way to a stony ridge and the view upriver toward Winston suddenly opened up. What Eugene saw next would haunt him for the rest of his life. The spill on Pond 2 had indeed torn open the dam, and the impoundment had unleashed millions of gallons of water and sludge in a matter of seconds. The wall of water had mounted, gathering force as it pressed through the narrow gorge consuming thousands of tons of refuse from every cliff and bank on its course downriver. At the oxbow at Twin Gap, where the river turned sharply through the ravine, the surge had slammed against the cliffs opposite and then followed the neck southward. It was enough to slow down the onslaught before it reached the old trestle, but even so, the angry waters hurled their violent and mangled payload onto the trestle's rugged steel girders.

And so there it was. A mountain of twisted metal, splintered buildings, wrecked fences, tractors, trucks, broken glass. Black lavalike mud spewing over it all, a grotesque mass piled up just short of the crossties. But the bridge had held. By the time Eugene could stop the train, they were within a hundred feet of it. He strained his eyes against the last rays of the ashen sky. Jammed and clotted and sealed tight with debris, he could see that the trestle had itself become a dam, and the last thing he saw before the dark set in completely was the tremendous murky lake that fanned out behind it. Should the trestle fail now, the magnitude of the surge would inundate the whole of Porterstown, and even more pressing in the mind of Eugene Gilbert was the fact that the train would go with it.

34

The jump was farther than Cody expected. He landed on a rocky ledge and the fall knocked the breath out of him. He shook it off, got up, and disappeared into a stand of scrubby pines that lined the ridge along South Mountain. He hadn't gotten far when he felt something, a presence, an urging that had become familiar, a counsel that he always followed. He stopped and listened and looked back.

He saw the lake that had formed and the trestle beyond it. He looked over the cliff. Even though the lake covered it now, he knew where he was. Down below him, on the shore immersed in the black depths, was the place where he was baptized. And on the trestle, where he saw her standing on that momentous day, the small silhouette of the train appeared. He knelt and watched. Whether it was in real time or some other place, he didn't know, but as the wind and water battered the trestle, he saw two expansive ethereal wings rising into the pewter sky, stretching across the river from bank to bank, a silver sun beaming between them, watching just as he was watching, until the train made it safely to the other side.

35

The caboose was the last to pass over. The trestle had held and the 49 continued its shaky ascent up the even steeper grade on the north side of the river. The cheers and shouts were deafening and echoed into the valley. Danny paused from the endless work of feeding the firebox and grabbed Eugene in a bear hug.

Eugene wiped the sweat from his face, "No time to celebrate yet. We may be clear of the river, but we still got five miles of precious track to navigate." The lines in his face softened momentarily before clamping down once again, this time with determination.

When Wayne returned to the cab to relieve Danny, Danny climbed up to the tender and then hopped to the roof of the freight car behind it. The doors opened toward the mountainside and people were jumping out and scrambling up to the top of the ridge unwilling to tempt fate a moment longer. The wind had finally died down. Thick clouds prevailed above him deepening the darkness, and it was hard to tell where the sky ended and the lake began. One thing was for certain. It stank. The coal, the sludge, the garbage. He could smell it now. Then he thought of the carcasses he had seen floating by in daylight–dogs, horses, cows, and worse. Yes, he had seen corpses. He shuddered to think of what the river would do to them in the days to come.

Above the din of wheels on rail, Danny thought he heard a voice. "Help us, help us," it cried. He peered into the night and followed the voice as the train passed through. He jumped from car to car straining to hear, trying to zero in. There! Two faces huddled along the river holding on a branch lodged in the mud. "Help us, please!"

He swung down to the landing on the back of the caboose. By the time he jumped off, he had overshot them. He ran back up the track until he heard them again. They were twenty feet down the embankment and it looked like the branch they held onto was giving way. It was a mother and her little girl, smeared in mud, and she was trying desperately to push her daughter up the cliff wall to safety.

"Hold still," Danny said. "You knock that branch loose and you'll have more trouble." It was wet and slippery but he thought he could make it. "You settle down. I'm coming after you." He took off his denim shirt and tied it around his waist then threw his legs over the edge in search of a foothold. To his relief, thick roots protruded at regular intervals, which got him down to within three feet of his charges. They watched him through hollow eyes. When he could go no further, he untied his shirt and said, "I'll take the young'un first. You old enough to climb?" The little girl nodded. "Okay then. When I toss you the end of my sleeve, I want you to grab it and hold on. You got that?" Danny dangled the shirt over the girl until it went taut. "Now we play a little game. You hold on as tight as you can and when you feel me pullin' don't let go, just keep holdin' on. You ready? Okay then." He wiped his brow and then pulled gently until he could feel the full weight of the little girl swaying in the air as he drew her up. "That's it. Just a little further. Keep holdin'." He reached out grabbed her cold wet body and the mother started to cry. "Don't worry, ma'am. She's just fine. I'll get her up the bank and then come back for you."

They climbed over the top and he sat the child on the wet grass. She was shivering and he wrapped her up in his shirt. "You'll be just fine right here. In a few minutes, I'll be back with your mama. You stay put."

He started back down the cliff and could hear the mother sobbing. "Calm down now. It's almost over. Just grab my hand. Can you reach it?" She stretched as far as she could but it wasn't far enough. "It's okay. We'll try again." When she reached out the second time, the branch cracked and she plunged into the water. Danny could see her thrashing and floundering, her open mouth sucking in water. He dove in and grabbed her by the back of her blouse before she went under. She grappled and wrestled with him until he thought they'd both drown. Finally she relaxed, exhausted, and he was able to find them a foothold near to where they had fallen in. "You go first," he said. "I'll come up behind you." Trembling, she patted around the dark cliff until she found something to grab onto and then hauled herself out of the water and began picking her way to the top. "Momma!" the little girl cried and she ran into her mother's arms.

Danny hoisted himself up and had just secured his boot on his first step to safety when an explosion shook the ground. He slipped and fell, and just before he hit the river, he saw the trestle collapse and disappear, and the wall of water behind it began to surge. It was the last thing he saw before being pulled under.

36

Amanda wasn't sure if she was dreaming or if she had died. It was when the water had filled the haymow and crept up and over the loft to the eaves that she felt herself surrender to it. Not to the black tide but to the profound and endearing presence that filled her now. On the barn roof, the moment the sun went down, a blanket of complete darkness had fallen over everything. No stars or moon shone, no streetlights or hearth light penetrated the night's absolute reign.

Earlier, before the farmhouse went under completely, she had shouted endlessly to Eppy, over and over until her throat was raw. The last thing she recalled before she fell into her other world was Eppy calling out, "The baby's comin'."

Amanda thought she had gone underwater too, same as Eppy. It sort of felt like that. She lay down on the roof and looked up. It must be water, she thought, because it began to shimmer, the way the ocean does when soft rays of the sun blow along its surface. But the light grew, not with the burnished light of day. It was silver, like tinsel on a tree. She sat up and saw it surround her, translucent and real. They were everywhere, a swarm, an army of light that was not quite light. Legions hovering over the lake, soaring up into the sky and down again, swooping here and there in their silent orchestration. Other light emerged, this time from the depths of the lake, green in color, ambiguous in shape, rising from the water and falling into the waiting wings of silver. Up and down they flew, across the banks and over the water. She watched them spin and dive and she hoped that soon they would come for her.

Then the trestle exploded. She saw the cloud of smoke press up the river, the breath of an angry dragon writhing in violent defeat. A roar and then the sound of rushing water receding in a great and awful riptide. The beast was retreating, and the angels, in fast pursuit, disappeared with it downriver towards Porterstown.

Ever so slowly Amanda's eyes began to see clearly. The sun had not yet risen above the ridge but its generous fire heated the air in the east with a gentle and swelling illumination over the bookstore.

The Yellow Bird had been spared and looked untouched. Beyond it, upriver to the north, the water was gone but so was everything else on the cliff, now bald and scoured and empty.

She turned and looked downriver. A soft fog hung over the valley, an immense cloud spreading over the water, the fields, and down into the hollows. The golden light of dawn drew near and the valley received it, catching its gilded rays in its misty folds. Above her, the sky had cleared and her heart ached to see the last star disappear into brightness.

A baby cried. Amanda looked toward the farmhouse. No. It was coming from behind her. She turned toward the hill and waited. The baby cried again. It was coming from the bookstore.

37

Amanda landed on the haymow floor with a thud. Everything was the same color, gray and wretched, even where the sun fell in patterns through the slats. She climbed down to the stalls and jumped into the mud. It squished between her toes. Her boots were gone, lost to the flood; so were her shoes and slicker. She stepped barefooted out of the barn and into the sunshine. Her tee shirt and jeans were torn to shreds and were covered in putrid slime. She rubbed her left hand. The knuckles were hot and swollen.

The path up to the bookstore had washed away and she picked her way through limbs and stones until she reached the hill that had escaped destruction. Except for a few wind-torn shingles missing off the roof and the trash that had blown all over the back lawn, the Yellow Bird stood fast and welcoming. Again the baby cried. She walked over the patio to the back porch. Her good hand trembled and rattled the knob in a clumsy effort to open the door.

"Who's there?" Came a voice from inside.

It was Eppy.

Amanda rushed into the front of the store and then stopped. There in the overstuffed chair, with the sun falling through the window panes, warm and comfortable, was Eppy, a soft blanket draped over her bare and muddy torso, her hand stroking the plump cheek of the baby at her breast.

"It's a boy," she said without looking up.

Amanda came closer and knelt beside them. He was beautiful. Moist and stained from birth, he sucked away, not a care in the world. Amanda touched his tiny pink hand and he grabbed her finger. She jumped and then she laughed. And Eppy laughed too. They laughed and laughed until they held each other and cried.

Amanda went into the kitchen for towels and saw the blood and afterbirth all over the floor. She poured water from a rain barrel into a wash pan and brought it back to the front room. Eppy tenderly washed the baby head to toe, then took a dishrag and folded it between his kicking legs, pinning it securely at either side. A piece of string dangled from the stub of umbilical cord still attached to his belly. He started to wail and she swaddled him in a towel and then gave him her breast.

"Have you got a box or somethin' we could use as a cradle?" she asked.

Amanda walked over to the crates of records in the corner and emptied one. The Victrola lid was open with the needle arm resting against the center of an old record. "You had time to play music?"

"Not me, but he did. He said it would help the baby come into the world a happy person."

"Who?"

"Cody. You know, Cody, the one that played at the revival with Morgan. He's the one that saved me." Eppy held the baby with one arm and laid a towel in the crate with the other. "I named him Cody," she said nesting him in the box. "Cody Morgan Greer. 'Cody' for the man that saved him, 'Morgan Greer' after his daddy."

Amanda looked surprised.

"Now you know he ain't the father but I think of Morgan as the real daddy anyway. And besides, we have talked about it. The reverend's goin' to marry us. That's how I know he ain't dead. God wouldn't save the baby just to kill the daddy. Nope, you'll see. Morgan's coming back."

They watched the baby sleep while she told Amanda the whole tale.

"The pains were comin' one after the other when the water

came creepin' up into the attic. Even if I could have squeezed out the window, I knew I wasn't able to climb to the roof. And here came the water, first to my knees, then up over my waist. I stood on a box to get as high up as I could but still it came up. I said my prayers one last time and decided it'd be quicker not to even try and hold my breath.

"That's when the window bust wide open and a man hollered out 'Anyone in there?' I called out and the next thing I knew he got me from up and under my arms and started kickin' and swimmin' toward the window, draggin' me along through the water. He went on through first but never let go of me. Then he flipped me on my back 'cause by that time the water had almost cleared the window and he thought I would drown. Then he floated me out and put me on a raft he had scotched out there against the chimney, a piece of plywood or somethin'. Then he started towin' us over the water by pulling on the phone line that ran from the house to the bookstore. When we got pretty close, we hit dry ground, and he sat me on the hill while he hauled the raft onto the grass." The baby started to cry, so Eppy lifted out of the crate and cradled him in her arms.

"He could see that my pains was comin' fast just then, so he carried me into the store and then helped me across to the backroom. I was headin' for the bathroom but didn't make it. My time had come, so I got down on the floor 'cause the pushin' urge came on me. The pain got just awful and I felt like givin' up, and I would have too, I was that worn out. But Cody wouldn't have it. He went to look for a flashlight. That's when I heard the music start to play. Amanda, I can't tell you how beautiful it sounded. It just filled the room and gave me hope. And it did the trick too, 'cause right then is when the baby's head crested. Cody kept hollerin' for me to push and I kept hollerin' for him to shut up. He made me mad which caused me to bear down one last time with all I got, and there he came, slidin' right out into Cody's hands. And oh did that baby wail and Cody said he was just like his mama and that made me laugh. 'A boy?' I asked. And he shined the flashlight between his little legs. A boy all right, and that made me cry.

Eppy leaned over to stroke the baby's cheek with her finger. "It was dark and hard to see, but when he bent over to give me the baby, he got real close, and I could tell that his face was all cut up. Like I say, it was dark but it looked pretty bad. I'm not sure if he even realized he was hurt. Once the baby took to suckin', I told him to go check in the mirror, which he did. When he came back he said it was nothin' but I didn't believe him and he wouldn't let me look. But I saw he had wrapped a rag clear around his head. He found a can of soda on the shelf and told me to drink it. I needed the sugar and the water, he said. He asked me if I could make it over to the chair in the front room, and I told him I could. He helped me up makin' sure I held the baby tight and he carried me over to the chair where he had piled some blankets since I was still bleedin'. It was a little before mornin', about the time we heard the last blast coming from down-river, when he said he was goin' to go for help."

She sighed deeply, then kissed the baby lightly on the forehead. "When you came to the door, I thought it'd be Cody."

The way she talked about him aroused Amanda's memory and she thought about all she had seen from the barn roof during the night. The story Eppy told made her remember something else, the way a dream is recalled from the periphery of the mind. She might have seen them coming out of the attic. Not Eppy so much, but him, and she remembered watching his light float along the water toward the Yellow Bird. She had thought it was Gabriel.

Morgan burst through the front door. His jaw went slack as he took it all in, Eppy in the chair muddy and bruised, and in her arms a sleeping baby boy. His brother Jesse came in behind him. Amanda noticed how much Morgan needed help walking. "Sit here next to Eppy," she said coaxing him in the chair. He and Eppy leaned into each other until their heads touched and they began to whisper. Then she caressed his face with the palm of her hand and he kissed her.

Jesse told Amanda what happened. He and his brothers had gone looking for Morgan and finally found him stranded down by the bend near Twin Gap, his foot pinned under a rock. When they dug him out they saw blood pumping out of his hand and realized he had lost his little finger. One of them made a tourniquet out of a piece of shirt and they carried him up the ridge. They were starting back up toward their farm when the trestle blew, and they were close enough to watch the whole lake empty into Porterstown.

It was morning by the time they reached the road that skirted Amanda's farm, Jesse said. A man was heading in the other direction and he stopped them. His head was covered in a crude bandage and blood was soaking through on the right side of his face. He was pointing to the bookstore. As he spoke, Morgan finally realized who it was and that he was telling them about Eppy. That she was all right. That the baby was born and he was all right too.

"Morgan is stubborn as a bull," Jesse told Amanda. "After he heard that, there was no swayin' him in any other direction but the Yellow Bird. I said I'd go with Morgan while my brothers took the man up to our farm so our mama could get a good look at his injury." Jesse looked over at his brother then said, "I imagine I'll have to separate these love birds before too long or Morgan may faint dead away from either longing or loss of blood."

38

They held the memorial in October.

Along the ridge, all of South Mountain burned bright with autumn leaves rustling against a clear and brilliant sky. It began at Piney Mount, the overlook halfway between Winston and Twin Gap, where the natural granite outcropping had for centuries provided a breathtaking panorama of the Chalahume River. Standing there, one could see past the oxbow at Twin Gap and beyond it all the way to the other side of Porterstown.

They brought flowers, and one by one each of them cast their blooms over the railing and watched them spin and soar in the gentle breeze, landing softly on the roiling water, floating downriver and out of sight.

The old 49 waited for them at the switch. She too was graced with flowers and other mementos placed with great and tender care to honor the ones they had lost only a few short months ago. Amanda saw a locket hanging from a gold chain, surrounded by holly and opened to a man's smiling face. Poems, rings, locks of hair. She saw a pair of small shoes and next to it the twenty-third psalm. And there were wreaths of cedar and hemlock festooned around the entire engine and every car, and everywhere there were thick drapes of black cloth.

The train pulled out and began the slow and silent procession toward Winston. The scarred valley was healing, yet the waft of decay indicated it had a long way to go. There was evidence of rebuilding along the river in Porterstown and cattle had resumed grazing along the cove. The trestle had been cleared out and word had come of funding to restore it.

As they continued up the ridge, Amanda spotted the Yellow Bird far below on the other side of the river, its metal roof flashing from the little hill in the sun. Beyond it was the farmhouse and barn, still abandoned.

The 49 pulled into the roundhouse and Eugene sounded a low mournful whistle. Bill was at the passenger door helping people down. As they disembarked and started across the lot to the widow Mahoney's field, a single voice began to sing "Will the Circle Be Unbroken". Some joined in, some did not. Some simply cried.

They gathered around the stage, the one that had delivered good cheer and fellowship at the Roundhouse Revival. Now great swags of black cloth draped across the top of the stage, gathered at intervals with large white rosettes. On either side, flags flew at half-mast.

Eppy held the baby against her shoulder and patted his back, her mother and father stood behind her. Next to Eppy were Morgan and Amanda, and next to them were Dehlia and Amanda's parents.

The reverend took the stage and approached the microphone. He looked out into the hundreds of faces he had grown to love and he found he couldn't speak. The tears filled his eyes. He bowed his head and said, "I am so sorry."

Bill came out and they embraced. In a spontaneous response, families, friends, strangers embraced one another, the moment too heavy to manage anything else. So many were gone. So many others missing. Still others were nursing wounds from hospital beds in distant states where they had been airlifted. Amanda thought of Gabriel. And she thought of Cody, and she wondered why he had not come.

Finally Joe opened his notes and began reading the list of the deceased. Slowly, when they heard the names, family members broke from the crowd and began walking toward the ridgeline where an enormous wooden cross had been erected, its silhouette overshadowing the impoundment below it, now in ruins, gaping and vacant.

"Lewis Bailey, 29, Twin Gap…Mary Lynn Bradshaw, 64, Porterstown…"

Eppy handed Morgan the baby, her eyes swollen and red. She took a bouquet of lilies from her father and she and her mother disappeared into the crowd.

Joe faltered when he read the name Danny Hollaway. He handed the list to Martha who continued the recitation. Then Joe joined Bill, Anna, and Wayne and they walked together toward the wooden cross holding flowers for their friend.

39

He hadn't been back since the flood. It took three hospitals in two states and countless specialists, but after several operations and as many infections, even *they* couldn't save his eye.

The weathered sign hung over the door, Yellow Bird. He was a fool for thinking he should go inside. He was afraid. He saw his reflection in the window glass and pulled the brim of his cap further down over his brow. Instead of sunglasses, he wore the eye patch. It was more honest. Yet he didn't think he would survive it if she looked at him and felt repulsed. He'd find out soon enough now.

He opened the door a crack and peered in. The bookstore was empty. The autumn days were getting shorter, but even in the dim and receding light, he could see more than he had his first time there, when he had carried Eppy into the storefront.

He heard something outside and around back. She must be out there. He could leave now and she'd never know, and he thought he would. But he didn't. He walked through the row of stacks. He saw a book of poems and took it off the shelf. He heard something again and thought she was coming in. Without looking he grabbed a couple more books. The backroom where he had helped Eppy deliver the baby was clean now but it still smelled sour and salty. He glanced out the window to the patio.

There she was. Her back turned to him, her dark brown hair thrust into a ponytail that swung back and forth as she stoked the small fire she had burning in the grill. She spun around and sat at the table and he backed away so she wouldn't see him.

Her features were as he imagined and yet they weren't. In these moments while he studied her, his worlds began to meld, one folding easily into the other. He had heard that her name was Amanda.

She suddenly looked up and into the window. Had she seen him? Her expression was at first open and inviting. Had she sensed his presence? Then her face turned hard and suspicious. The moment had arrived.

He opened the door and walked onto the patio. Her green eyes were piercing and the way they caught the light startled him. They were strange and familiar all at once, a trick of the deepening sky or more likely the drifting of his own imagination. He took off his cap.

"The door was unlocked, so I let myself in," he managed to say. He stood before her and allowed the thorough inspection. He watched a million thoughts cross over her face. She's wondering about me, he thought, relieved that the mysterious thread between them was still holding.

"I'm just passing through," he said, "and was lookin' for somethin' to read." She was tapping her lip now and although he fought against it, he could feel himself smile.

"We're closed," she said.

She was drinking beer so he took a chance. "I'd like to pay for a couple of books, and some of that beer if you're sellin' it." It worked. She relaxed and led him into the store. He placed the books on the counter. Then he read their titles and winced.

When he heard her laugh right out loud, spontaneous and pure, he wanted to kiss her. But he knew he couldn't, he couldn't tell her anything. Not yet. She needed to find it for herself. She needed time, that's all, and he would give it to her. He took the books and beer and walked out the door to his truck parked across the road. He opened the door, sat behind the wheel, and waited.

Eternity can be defined as the time is takes for the fates to play their cards. The sun had set, the store was dark, and she hadn't bothered to turn on the lights. He closed his eyes and began to think it was all a mistake. Heaven was heaven. Earth was earth. That's all there was to it. Nothing more. Then a very real and staggering fact descended upon him: they would never touch. They were never meant to. He was the fool after all.

She tapped him on the shoulder, "Gabriel?"

"No."

"Cody?"

She knew.

He got out and leaned on the truck next to her. Recognition and pain and then relief coursed between them. He found her hand and she wove her fingers through his. Time stopped. "You okay?" he asked.

"I don't know. I'm trying not to freeze up," she said. "What about you?"

"Same. It's crazy, huh? How much do you know?"

"About you? Everything that matters. I was sure of it. Now with you right here, finally, after all this time, I feel like I don't know much at all."

"We'll start over."

He handed her a beer and they walked back into the Yellow Bird. Soon a candle shone in the window and the soft music of the Victrola floated through the air, up and up to the highest heavens.

Yellow bird, yellow bird
Won't you come by here
And play where cedars grow
Yellow bird, yellow bird
Won't you open up
Your box of lace and snow

Yellow bird, yellow bird
Have you picked the fruit
From beds laid so sincere
Yellow bird, yellow bird
I intend to wait
To hear your footsteps near

Do you tarry in the orchard dear
Or by the silver pond
Do you toss your coins upon the deep
Well wishes sailing on

Give up your jar of lion's bane
Your comb where honey flows
Give up your promise to hold dear
The riches and the gold

I've come with news of distant dreams
That beckon down the road
But I cannot bear to go that way
And leave you here alone

When did you come to care for me
How long were ribbons tied
Upon the tender grafted limbs
Where wounded sparrows died

Don't tell me that you'll wait for me
And harbor all you know
For the time of waiting passed this way
A long long time ago

Yellow bird, yellow bird
Won't you let me reap
The sorrow that you sow
And plant it where the air is free
And the wild apples grow

Will you look for me along the heath
In places hard to find
And after tears of circumstance
Won't you share my apple wine

Yellow bird, yellow bird
Come and take my hand
Your burden I have borne
And lay your alabaster box
Upon my crown of thorns

The End

Acknowledgments

MY DEEPEST THANKS TO:

My family who never fails to inspire and ground me.

Dave for joining me on life's long journey.

Liza and Josie who from their first day have
filled me with love and gratitude.

Todd and Shawn for enriching our family circle.

Mia and Jack who always remind me to play.

Papaw whose memories of East Tennessee
ignited the idea for this story.

Sharon, the repository of Memaw's tales,
for keeping the family stories alive.

My sisters, Lois and Pam, for all our childhood memories.

My godmother Carol for her enthusiasm and
support from the beginning.

Amy, Lois, and Elaine, my circle of friends, for being there.

Eser, Sally, Marjo, Zaw, Lisa, Carlotta, Nancy, and my friends at
Maret School for their astute, kind, and generous help.

My book club sisters, Elizabeth, Jo, and Judy, who braved the first
draft and asked the hard questions.

Kendal, my local public librarian, who accepted the first
edition into the library's local author collection.

AND ESPECIALLY TO:

My father who gave me the heart to keep trying.

My mother who never stopped believing.

www.ingramcontent.com/pod-product-compliance
Lightning Source LLC
Chambersburg PA
CBHW071943170626
46813CB00005B/1812